HE BET THE FARM

He Bet the Farm

MIKE CONKLIN

Write Stuff Publishing

© *Copyright 2024*

ISBN: 978-1-958943-99-1 (Paperback)

ISBN: 978-0-9995166-9-5 (Ebook)

Published by Write Stuff Publishing

Chicago, Illinois

Manuscript formatting and production by Fort Raphael Publishing Co.

Cover design by Paul Stroili, Touchstone Graphic Design

Contents

1	The Hook	1
2	School Bells	4
3	Looking Ahead	7
4	Cutting It Short	13
5	The Great Migration	16
6	Breaking Bad News	19
7	Decisions, Decisions	22
8	Starting Blocks	27
9	More Than a Teacher	30
10	Getting to Know You	35
11	Soldiering On	43
12	Marshall's Plan	49
13	His Last Stand	53
14	Land of Lincoln?	57
15	School Daze	64
16	Homework 101	68
17	In Their Spare Time	72

18	Raising Stakes	76
19	Library Overdue	81
20	Digging In	88
21	Report Card	92
22	Status Report 1	95
23	Status Report 2	98
24	Moving On Up	101
25	Underground Railroad Story by Students	103
26	Breaking Through	109
27	Here's David	113
28	The Plots Thicken	117
29	News Bulletin	120
30	What Holiday Break?	123
31	Mr. Clutch	128
32	Good & Bad News	132
33	Closer Looks	135
34	Next Step	138
35	Start The Presses	141
36	Library Pulse Beat	145
37	Victory, Sort Of	148
38	Digging In	152
39	Sorting It Out	156
40	Beating The Odds	161

41	Family Reunion	168
42	Here Comes the Parade	173
43	Call Him Curious	177
44	Jackpot!!	183
45	Discovery	188
46	Whoops	190
47	Hoop Dreams	193
48	The Fix Is On	195
49	Book Ends	200
50	Stop the Presses	203
51	Jimmy's Future	209
52	Commencement	213
53	Sweet Sorrow	217

| *About The Author* | 220 |
| *Acknowledgements* | 221 |

Chapter 1

The Hook

His exit from the Princess Riverboat Casino came with a smile and great relief. He could just as easily be walking off a plank into the Ohio River. The gambling gods hovering above bailed him. Never again would he catch the fever. Definitely.

What seemed like a pleasant, first-time diversion on a sunny Saturday afternoon---checking out the Princess Casino, and its sparkling new, heavily promoted sports betting parlor---turned into a near-disaster after several successful bets set the stage.

One hundred dollars that Illinois would come within 15 points of Clemson; $300 that Alabama would squash Central Florida by 20 points; and $400 that Brigham Young wouldn't come within 12 against Oregon?

He shouldn't be doing this. He couldn't afford it. But all he needed was one big payoff that would put him in the black.

But almost everything he touched was turning into shit. It was as if some outside force had taken possession of his body. Never mind that he knew very little about schools outside Indiana and their football teams.

How could he ever explain to Milly, his wife, that he dropped nearly $3,500 betting on college football games in one after-noon? Things were tight enough with her working as a cook for the local elementary school, with three kids in college, and him trying to squeeze returns from a modest, but heavily mortgaged farm.

How could anyone be this dumb? He replayed the sequence in his mind. He started with a win, Indiana upsetting Tennessee. This was the original matchup that held his interest and lured him to this first-ever Princess visit. He spent $50 on Indiana winning by more than the 9-point spread, which it did 28-13, and another $50 on the two rivals combining for more than 40 points, which they also did---barely.

Well, hell, no problem.

"Easy money," he said to himself as he cashed his winning stubs at the ticket window. "This ain't so tough. I just won me a day's pay, at least.

"Nice going," said the cashier. "You obviously know your football."

"What else is on the scoreboard?" he answered.

Notre Dame, Boston College, Northern Illinois, Central Florida, Minnesota, Utah, New Mexico State, Louisiana Tech, Western Kentucky. The schools and games he wagered on blurred past like locomotives in the night as he bought ticket after ticket---almost all losers, compounded by trying to recoup losses each time by raising stakes.

His original golden touch turned into brass knuckles. He was rolling down a hill and headed for a cliff. He could see it, but couldn't stop.

Finally, mumbling and cursing to himself, he managed to pull away from the giant scoreboard in the Princess Casino's betting parlor. Never again, he said to himself. Never mind that sports betting now legal in Indiana. The boat, docked on the Ohio River, was practically in his backyard in the state's far, southern tip.

He had phoned home to say he would be late. He gave Milly some malarky about a farm sale and picking up some needed bargains. He could get by not mentioning his losses, at least until the credit card statements materialized later in the month.

As he started toward the door fumbling for car keys, thoroughly depressed, and inventing lame excuses, he pulled out a forgotten ticket purchased during his frenzied betting fever---Colorado State vs. North Texas State.

Since the contest was still in the fourth quarter, Ernie leaned against the bar near the exit to watch its conclusion on a TV monitor. Just like many teams that passed through his wallet that day, it was two schools he'd never heard of, but who cared? At this point, it could be Podunk State vs. Moo U.

The score was 35-20, with Colorado State leading. Ernie was about to tear up another losing ticket. Then, on the last play of the contest, the North Texas quarterback, whose name he would quickly forget, tossed an 82-yard bomb to a receiver, whose name he also would quickly forget, for a touchdown. Colorado State 35, North Texas 27.

More important than who won or lost: North Texas beat the oddsmakers' projected 12-point deficit and the two teams surpassed their 40-point total line for the contest.

Quickly he counted his payback. His total for the day still a loss, but only $75 due to this last, breathtaking result. He could live with that. It sure the hell beat $3,500 in the hole. The wife would be irritated, but she'd get over it. She'd never know how close he'd come to disaster before North Texas State came to his rescue.

He grinned as he pulled out of the parking lot in his mud-splattered pickup truck. Just 20 minutes ago, he was saying, "never again." Now, he was replaying how he could have reversed at least two other losing outcomes.

Maybe I just need to set limits, he thought. Would he make a return trip to the Princess someday? That was the best bet of the day.

Chapter 2

School Bells

The start of a new academic year on a college campus is a rush. Friends are reunited, gossip gets exchanged, students analyze new professors, professors analyze new students, upperclass students inspect the freshmen, new wardrobes are on display, no one's fallen behind in their studies, and the weekday pace in local pubs quickens.

It's no different for Harrison College, a small, liberal arts school in a rural community with the same name in deep southern Indiana. This would be my fourth year in the English Department, where I teach both writing and contemporary literature courses. Oh, before I forget, my name is Phillip Doyle, or Flip for short. I tend to be pretty informal---unconventional?--- when it comes to titles.

My undergraduate days were spent at Lake Forest College on Chicago's North Shore. I was editor of the school paper and spent summers working on a small, weekly newspaper, which, little did I know then, was good training

Harrison is my first real college teaching job in the U.S. After receiving an MFA in creative writing from the University of Iowa, I spent a year in China teaching at Xiamen University.

The students there were as eager to learn about American pop culture as they were writing.

A pre-Covid year abroad was not what I had in mind initially, but it was my best option when no college jobs of consequence materialized for me in the U.S The university was located on the South China Sea in a city of 4.3 million. In the U.S., the population would've made it one of the three largest cities. In China, it barely cracked the top 25---and it was everything the Asian nation is not supposed to be in the minds of Americans---white sand beaches, clear skies, fancy high-rise hotels, friendly relations with Taiwan, and a bustling nightlife.

The year spent in China became valuable. Later, at Harrison, I got tapped to use my Asian contacts to forge an exchange program between our schools. China was "hot" in U.S. higher ed circles. College officials salivate over the prospect of enrolling Asian students. Typically, they do not need financial aid and that's a good thing. Often their parents become big donors.

The only other Chinese footprint on our campus at the time I joined Harrison, belonged to Li Jei, a biology professor. He grew up in Duluth, Minnesota, and never set foot in Asia. His parents ran a popular restaurant.

To my knowledge, I was the only Harrison staffer to actually set foot in China. My stock skyrocketed more when the first class of Chinese students I helped recruit included several talented basketball players. Good basketball players are never a bad thing in Indiana.

With that experience under my belt, and also building an innovative writing program, the school's ambitious president, Jonathan Casey, rewarded me with an unprecedented---for a non-tenured teacher---contract extension. The promotion came with a healthy pay raise and a new title---Long Term Teaching Professional (LTTP)---a status that left the school's Old Guard scratching their heads.

Never mind that the "professional" in my new title consisted of summers writing obituaries for that small weekly.

Just as pleasing for me was this: Due to my sliver of experience and title, I qualified to move from my tiny office in Durham Hall's basement to something more commodious on the second floor. Initially flanked by the building's furnace and men's room, the move meant no more sounds of thermostat-induced clanking pipes in the winter or farting, grunting and toilet flushing wafting through my walls.

It was several days before the start of Harrison's classes when the president's secretary called to tell me he wanted to have coffee the next day to discuss "a few things."

This was not a total surprise. A private conversation with President Casey occurred at the start of each of my Harrison years. I'm confident not every teacher got the pleasure. The president seemingly had anointed me, with several other, young, hand-picked teachers he recruited, as his personal catalysts for a campus Renaissance in and out of the classrooms.

This took some end runs and other diversionary, bureaucratic-loving tactics around the Methuselahs in control of the school's academic side. They were under the thumb of the Office of The Dean. It was their committees that gave a thumbs-up or thumbs-down to new classroom courses, scheduling, and syllabus approvals. They were not about to loosen the grip---or vision---of their tenure-laced, Ivy-covered academia.

No wonder Harrison ranked among the top 10 liberal arts schools for "falling asleep in the classroom," a spurious poll published several years ago in one of those frisky higher ed chronicles.

Chapter 3

Looking Ahead

"Was it a good summer for you," asked President Casey, as he moved from behind his desk to take a more comfortable chair facing me. "Don't you spend time in Arizona, working on Mary's projects?"

The president was wired. Even though we had separate quarters in the same off-campus apartment building, he knew Mary Jagger, an assistant professor in sociology, and I were more than *casual* neighbors. The president, I knew, was just making polite conversation before he hit me over the head with a project.

Mary's specialty in sociology was Hispanic/Latino migration and Mexican border issues. While that may sound a bit incongruous for a small, liberal arts college like Harrison in southern Indiana, the fact is---she demonstrated repeatedly---migrants have become a growing, dynamic and significant demographic force in states like Indiana, Ohio, Illinois, Nebraska and Iowa.

She proved and reported this with a variety of innovative field projects. Her students do everything with migrants from detasseling corn and riding in market-bound trucks loaded with pigs to after-school tutoring and coaching soccer. They also organize field trips, find part-time jobs, and plan clinics.

Her Summers off? They're devoted to work in Arizona and the Phoenix area, where she earned her PhD at Arizona State. There she fell in with a core of social workers, concerned academicians and Catholic priests---Vincentian---operating schools, dormitories, soup kitchens and transitional services for mostly indigent migrants.

I've joined her for a month of volunteer work the last few summers, mostly teaching English. Rewarding, but with an average July temp something like 105 degrees, a little on the fry side.

Mary was a rising star at Harrison. She had been a guest speaker at a half-dozen or so national clinics and conferences in only three years at Harrison. She found her niche and, though we made only passing references and jokes over her growing celebrity, it was obvious she was headed for bigger things than our small school in rural Indiana could provide.

Where did I fit in? My star was still looking for liftoff.

On the other hand, I was doing OK for someone who sort of snuck in academia's backdoor. With only a Master of Fine Arts (MFA) degree and no doctorate like Mary, I probably was damn lucky to have my teaching situation---and a president like Casey who had my back.

In my MFA specialty, creative writing, it likely would take a best-selling novel to get upwardly mobile in the job market. That, or a positive guest shot on CBS's "60 Minutes" or maybe used as an expert for a PBS-TV documentary. Hell, I'd take being quoted as an "expert" in a Chronicle of Higher Education story.

But meanwhile, I had stumbled into Harrison exactly at the right time. Sometimes it's better to be lucky than good!

Yes, the new president, never to be mistaken for Mr. Chips, had anointed me and a handful of other ambitious, new faculty members to shake things up, drag his mostly moribund faculty---kicking and screaming---into the 21st century and in some cases the 20th century.

This meant new courses and new classroom techniques. Or, in the language of the unconverted, new "pedagogical approaches." As it turned out, my unfiltered classroom projects and lifestyle fit perfectly into President Casey's thinking. Timing is everything.

In my first year, I had helped Harrison make that connection with Xiamen. No small deal. Then, as a follow-up the next year, I introduced a newly-created, first time writing class---formed over the objections of the academic dean: "Our job is to educate, we're not a vocational school," was his response behind my back.

President Casey also was big on bettering relations between the college and non-college community in Harrison, or Town & Gown as he labeled those efforts. The atmosphere wasn't exactly North and South Korea, but very little appreciation for each other's world took place. Only a handful of local kids enrolled in the college and few town residents attended our events. The campus seemed to be regarded as some kind of castle inhabited by aliens.

In turn, faculty rarely participated in civic affairs and community social events, and as a rule, did not patronize local merchants. No faculty had ever served on Harrison's city council or library board. Serious shopping was done in Evansville or Indianapolis, but little faculty money changed hands in Harrison stores---outside of the college's bookstore. Also, a good share of faculty sent their kids to out-of-town private secondary schools.

President Casey encouraged everyone on the campus to get involved---city council committees, park boards, Red Cross, library boards, school board or whatever. I honored the initiative thusly: I joined the local Rotary Club. Seriously.

As far as anyone figured, a Harrison educator never before belonged to the organization. Too pedestrian, I guess. Weren't these the good old boys who wore Fez caps? Never mind the faculty likely was not aware this organization was a huge contributor to worldwide educational programs at all levels.

I didn't know what to expect with my membership and, though I had to be the youngest member of the local group, it proved to be quite a convivial experience. Almost anybody who was anyone in Harrison---mayor, public board members, police chief, pastors, lawyers, retired farmers, etc.---belonged.

Sitting at the same table, this is how I first met Newt Ames, publisher of the weekly, local *Hoosier-Record* newspaper. Together we hammered out a way for my students to begin writing feature content to contribute to his grossly understaffed publication. In fact, this led to an advanced writing class devoted exclusively to that exercise.

In the process, individual internships were established to give students valuable writing experiences. This also provided several adventures, including one memorable project in which we became entangled in helping solve a 50-year-old mystery surrounding a local, unsolved death.

President Casey, recounting my adventures, said, "Flip, you've created a lot of excitement since arriving. More than most. Let's hope things slow down a bit for you this school year. There's still a lot to accomplish at Harrison, as we know, but I don't want to create distractions for you and your teaching. Any more than I have to, that is."

Here it comes, I figured. Did he want me in the bullpen to put out new fires? What are some of the projects he would be working on this school year?

"China and our exchanges remain ongoing, and that's a good thing," he said. "In fact, some of our efforts to form a Chinese Studies major are coming together nicely. They should be fully in place and ready to go a year from now. That's my goal.

"The big thing? That's our capital drive for the new science center. Between you and me, and a few others, we expect to hit our target on time at the end of September. We'll make an announcement at homecoming.

"As things progress, there may be some added Chinese funding in the mix. We hope to have construction work done on the new center in time to start a year from now, but that may be wishful thinking on my part. Eventually, this will mean re-configuring courses to adapt to the superior facilities."

He paused to take a deep breath, then continued: "Oh, and I almost forgot. eSports."

"Huh?" That was my response. I wasn't sure if I said it out loud or just to myself.

"Eventually, I want an eSports program started here. By the next academic year. It would be a perfect complement to the new science center."

"A what? I never really heard of it unless you mean video games. At Harrison? As a course?"

The president went on to explain the competitive formats used in the competition, though he was a bit hazy on particulars and how it was organized. Since competition was outside the purview of the National Collegiate Athletic Association (NCAA), the teams representing schools were set up as clubs with loose---as of now---rules.

"There are three things that really appeal to me," said the president, his eyes widening as he sat up straighter in his chair.

"For one it's a natural outgrowth of interest in video technology. I see us eventually building some science courses around this. Maybe make it a minor. "For another, eSports are growing like crazy. Last time I noticed there are something like 200 colleges with teams. Probably more. For a small, private liberal arts college like us, it would look very progressive for us to be a part of this wave.

"And it's a great equalizer. Lots of parity. You've got the big universities---Ohio State, UCLA, Missouri, Illinois, Purdue---with programs, but three of what are considered the top five in eSport rankings are small schools few have heard of---Kansas Wesleyan, Northwood, Maryville. Only two other Indiana schools---Purdue and Rose Hulman Institute of Technology---have programs.

"Why not? Low overhead compared to what Harrison shells out for football and basketball."

There was a noticeably longer-than-usual pause in our conversation. This was delicate turf for me. Surely, President Casey wasn't trying to get me in the eSport mix? Nahhh! My last exposure to electronic games was Pac Man at the local bowling alley.

But I could see my advanced writing class doing a feature on eSports at Harrison College for the *Hoosier-Record*. Surely it would interest readers of the weekly newspaper.

I could hear it now: "Another of them crazy things they're doing at the college" would be the likely response. Newt would love it, doing something that was beyond re-writing press releases.

While coming out as an extracurricular sport would not be that difficult to establish, maybe the real story would be this: How in the world could gaming courses get on the board as academic? How could they navigate the murky waters of approval from Dean Brunk, our esteemed (stuffy? pompous?) academic dean who thought high technology was his auto-matic garage door opener?

At the very least, this was not a battle I wished to help President Casey fight beyond a story in the local newspaper. On the other hand, my students would gobble it up. He seemed to sense my hesitancy as our meeting broke up. It would be good to simply teach my courses. No more solving local mysteries.

You think?

Chapter 4

Cutting It Short

From the sublime to the ridiculous. Well, that might be a bit harsh. I had one more pre-school meeting and, at the very least, this one figured to be shorter than my meetup with President Casey---and, as it turned out, even shorter than I hoped.

It was with Prof. William Schackelford, the English Department Chair and the longest-serving Harrison teacher in such a position both as a professor and department head.

Our meeting was a ritual every chairperson experienced with his teaching staff a few days before the start of a new school year. The chair would relay thoughts and suggestions from Dean Brunk and, in turn, listen to any thoughts or suggestions from his department's faculty.

Generally, it ended there. Everyone slipped quietly back into the way they'd always went about their work.

The English Department had five full-time teachers and two part-time adjuncts. My Writing 1 and Writing 2 courses were new. The work was glorified journalism. We aimed to write five 900-word feature pieces that, if on the right topics, could easily be run in a magazine or newspaper---which they occasionally were in the local, weekly *Hoosier-Record* thanks to my Rotary connection with Newt Ames, the publisher-editor-reporter.

I also taught two American literature classes during the academic year, one dealing with creative nonfiction ("In Cold Blood," "Rumor of War," "Seabiscuit," etc.) and the other straight fiction ("The Grapes of Wrath," "The Catcher in The Rye," "To Kill a Mockingbird," etc.).

All my courses were groundbreakers for Harrison, which never before ventured beyond 19th-century literature under the dean's tight grip. Due to the flu bug, he missed the general meeting in which voting took place on my new classes. Thus, his loyal troops did not know which way to go---and, in their leader-less state of confusion, my proposals got approved by slim margins.

Undoubtedly Dean Brunk eventually would've found a way to squash them after their first year, but he had a problem. The courses were popular. Each drew maximum enrollment, with waiting lists, and the dean, no dummy when it came to bottom lines, got painted into an unhappy corner.

When it came to my department meetings with Professor Schackelford, things were purely perfunctory and relaxed. The professor, who came to Harrison a year before Brunk, was a loyal ally of the dean, rubber stamping his every decision. That did not necessarily make him a bad guy. I'm sure he was a warm and fuzzy grandfather.

When prodded, old "Schack," softer than ever at this stage of life, had great stories to tell. Whether he knew it or not, for me he was an unwitting source of valuable school history in our chats. You never know when the tiniest detail could become important, and academia, if nothing else, is loaded with tiny details.

Once, leaning over and almost in a whisper, he confided to me that his technical know-how did not go beyond email (as if I didn't know). It was not lost on me that this round of pre-schoolyear meetings was quite a contrast: I'd gone from the possibility of Harrison adopting a video gaming program in the first session to, just 24 hours later, learning my department chair was, for all practical purposes, technically illiterate.

eSports? They wouldn't have a chance with this immediate superior if things ever came to a faculty vote. This blank spot made Professor Schackelford especially appreciative of Bea, his department secretary, who wisely took care of his record keeping and email with whatever technology was needed. Deep down, I think he liked me, too, but this probably had more to do with my overflow English classes. Professor Schackelford, like any good administrator, was aware of the growing waiting lists for my classes.

Good numbers never hurt. By now, my small requests and suggestions to the department chair were getting rubber-stamp approvals.

But halfway through our meeting, Bea came in with an important call for him. "Doctor Schackelford, your physician's office is on the telephone---line 2," she said. "Apparently, they have an opening an hour from now due to an unexpected schedule cancellation. The slot is yours if you can make it."

Turning to me, he said: "Phillip, do you mind if we cut this meeting short? I've been trying to get on my doctor's schedule for a while. I need to get rid of this cough I've had for several weeks. I'm drowning in over-the-counter syrups. My home Covid tests have all turned up good, so there's that."

No problem. We agreed to pick it up at a later date in the semester. By then, I'd be deep into what hopefully would be an undisturbed class term.

"Keep up the fine work," he said, as we departed. "You've got a bright future."

Little did I know.

Chapter 5

The Great Migration

The start of a new school year at Harrison College, like most institutions of higher learning, really starts in August, several weeks before first classes convene. Everyone arrives in waves.

Student workers, or board jobbers, precede everything. They toil at cleaning dining hall kitchens, sweeping out dormitory rooms, filing books and periodicals in the library, etc. About the same time the Generals, nickname for the Harrison sports squads that compete in the fall—football, cross-country, tennis, soccer---are in a rush to start pre-season training.

The campus parking lots, nearly empty all summer, suddenly become crowded with students allowed to move into dormitories early. This wave includes upper-class students who will be dormitory proctors. There are no reserved spots. More than a few bumpers and doors get scraped with everyone jockeying for prime locations.

This year, in a homey touch created by President Casey as part of his Town & Gown initiative, local Boy Scout troops have been hired to help with unloading cars and overall traffic control on the campus's arrival day for freshmen. The newbies arrive five days earlier than the regular student body for orientation that is mandatory for first-year students.

Typically, the first-year students fall into two classifications.

Secretly, they're sobbing or extremely nervous. With the exception of overnight summer camps, they've almost never lived anywhere but with good old Mom, Dad, and siblings. Now they're sleeping in close quarters with a total stranger. Will he or she snore?

Or secondly, they cannot get away from their home and parents fast enough---practically pushing Mom and Dad out the door. They breeze through orientation. They do pay closest attention when visiting fraternity and sorority houses but learn no one is allowed to join until the second semester. Some will have fake IDs and hit the pubs.

The freshmen get numerous tours. For some, the visit to the library will be the one and only time during the school year they set foot in the building. Also, after the upper classes arrive, an all-school convocation is held in Harrison's mammoth, historical William Fletcher Chapel. Music is provided by the school's student chamber group.

The makeup of the student body?

Harrison, being a four-year, residential liberal arts college in far southern Indiana, draws the biggest share of its students from the Hoosier state---mostly the Indianapolis area---and northern Kentucky. In no particular order, parts of Illinois, Michigan and Ohio significantly contribute, too. Almost every student lives in a dormitory or fraternity (there are four) or sorority house (three).

Harrison is like hundreds of other undergraduate-only schools in America: four years and out the door. It's expensive---close to $40,000 per year without scholarships and grants---and almost no one graduates without loans following them out the door.

President Casey watches enrollment numbers like a hawk. He is trying to break new ground in larger Midwestern cities such as Chicago, Louisville, Detroit, and Columbus (Ohio). About

15-20% of the 1,500 students are Asian, African-American, or Latino/Hispanic. A handful of locals, or non-traditional students, live off campus.

Chapter 6

Breaking Bad News

Joey Burke is a local, of sorts. He lives on a farm with his parents and two siblings approximately 15 miles from the Harrison campus. He went to high school at a smaller, more rural location than in the City of Harrison. He rode a school bus to his classes until his senior year, when his parents provided him with a 10-year old, beat up Hyundai for him to get to his two part-time, after-school jobs.

Joey loved his first year at Harrison College. Despite the close proximity of his farm home to the campus, his parents scraped enough money together including a few loans from the local bank---to allow him to live in a dormitory.

He couldn't wait to return for his second year and be reunited with Tim Jackson, his freshman roommate from Evansville. Joey's full-time summer job---driving 41 miles round trip every weekday to work in a stifling turkey processing plant---made him more determined than ever to get his degree from Harrison and get out of southern Indiana.

Too bad there wouldn't be a second year at Harrison College for Joey. That news hit him like a thunderbolt.

Just three days before packing and driving off to his dormitory, he knew something was amiss when he came downstairs and walked into the kitchen for breakfast. His Dad, Pete, was sitting at the table drumming his fingers. With his days at home numbered before leaving for school, he thought his Dad simply wanted to join him for breakfast before attacking his daily farm chores.

But Pete's smile---what there was to it---clearly was tight, forced. Obviously, he was there to deliver bad news, and he was: "Son, you're gonna have to quit college. We can't afford it no more."

Tossing numbers, credit ratings, mortgage payments, and a variety of other financial concepts that sailed over his head, Joey was told by his Dad---his Mom was already at work in the local high school cafeteria---that the Burkes were about to lose their 225-acre farm to the bank and other creditors.

They had 30 days to get things in order and move if they wanted to avoid an unseemly, embarrassing public eviction---furniture on the lawn, bankrupt credit cards, collector at the door, etc.

"The math just ain't there," Pete summed up for his son. "Our bills and interest payments are too much. Thought we could make it another year, but we ain't. Every projection I've seen for what crops will bring this fall won't carry us.

"We're going broke."

There was complete silence. Then, Joey wanted to know about his sister Brittney, entering her senior year at Indiana State, and his brother Jimmy, a star basketball player at the University of Lexington in Kentucky.

"Jimmy's going to be OK," was the answer. "We've been told he's getting a full-ride this year at Lex. Even getting a summer job. The basketball coach likes him that much. He did have a good season last year, and this'll cover tuition and room and board for this year. He just needs to keep playing good. Oh, and keep up his grades.

"Brit's a different story. No scholarships, but your grandparents are pitching in. She's too close to graduating. It's likely she can walk right into a teaching job. That's what she wants to do anyway.

"It kills me we can't do anything for you right now, son, but Harrison ain't cheap. When Brittney's out, maybe we can do something and get you back there. Or find a cheaper school. Them online schools might work."

Pete's best plan: Joey goes back to work at the turkey plant, saves his money, and returns to Harrison as soon as he can, but lives at home and eliminates room and board.

"That's about the best we can do now."

Joey thought he could squeeze in a few classes at the two-year community college. The credits would transfer when---not if---he re-enrolled at Harrison.

Right now, that seemed to be miles and miles in the future.

Chapter 7

Decisions, Decisions

Now that it was a wrap for me with the president and English Department Chair, there was another new school year ritual that needed to be observed. A highly informal one, though.

On the eve of the first day of classes, Mary and I typically visited Whitey's for a few drinks. This was topped off afterwards at one of our adjoining apartments---and maybe you can guess the finale.

For the uninitiated, Whitey's is a rural bar on the historic Tippecanoe River that winds its way through the State of Indiana, eventually emptying into the Ohio River. The saloon's wizened proprietor, Whitey, was a great source for local color. "There ain't a whole lot happening in Harrison," he'd tell anyone, "but it all gets told here."

This was especially true at the start of a new school year when too many students hit the town's watering holes. You couldn't help but bump into them. Between those wanting to argue over a poor grade when they spotted you, or tipsy coeds more than willing to do what it took to improve a grade, everything spelled trouble for a faculty member.

But at Whitey's you were as likely to bump into the mayor and farmers as you were small business proprietors and tradesmen. Occasionally someone in leather on a motorcycle would wander onto the premises, but that never led to trouble.

Never mind that Whitey's was a good five miles from Harrison. This was the community's "adult" bar, the older generations driven there by students who flooded the taverns in town.

Card games and pool table only. None of the fancy electronic games found mainly in arcades. eSports would never have a chance here.

Once I counted a half-dozen Rotarians patronizing Whitey's at the same time, prompting my suggestion---rejected---that club committee meetings be held here.

In addition to clergy, always conspicuously (to me) absent were any of my college teaching colleagues. Unquestioningly the atmosphere was too low brow. Didn't bother me, nor Mary.

Our professions enhanced us in Whitey's eyes, and that was always good for a free beer. As college professor patrons, we had become almost mythical to him. He loved to join us for a few minutes in a booth to get the latest college gossip and any other nuggets he couldn't mine from regular clientele. I always felt flattered when, occasionally, he jotted down a note or two after something we said.

After joining us for a few minutes, bitching about how the new Princess Casino boat on the nearby Ohio River was stealing his regulars, he jumped up to tend to business. "Good to see you two again," he said. "Bring some friends next time."

After Whitey walked away, Mary delivered surprising news, making sure I got it first.

"This may be my last year at Harrison, Flip," she blurted. "We've got to talk. I need some input from you."

Gulp. There was a very pregnant pause. No double meaning intended.

While we had briefly broached this topic in the past - that one, or both of us, moving upward and onward from Harrison, we had settled into a comfort zone waiting for career decisions to arrive. In fact, the upcoming school year looked especially comfortable with our innovative (for Harrison) teaching approaches gaining credence with peers.

Finally, I broke the silence, and asked, "What gives? Offers?"

"Exactly," Mary answered. "Well, one offer and another dynamite opportunity may be available.

"The first possibility is Kansas State, the university in Manhattan, Kansas. My home state, not that it makes a difference. They've got a big agricultural department there, with lots of specialty majors---agribusiness, agronomy, food technology, animal science, dairy science. Even winemaking.

"They're one of the few universities---probably something to do with their location---that acknowledges immigration as a growing dynamic impacting farming practices and yields. Not in a bad way, either. Whether it's something that's here to stay and, because of that, needs to be specifically studied."

Where would Mary fit in? She continued.

"The school wants to develop a line of courses that specifically focus on immigration's impact and, especially, in the Upper Midwest with Spanish speakers.

There's nothing there like that now, or in other universities with agriculture programs.

"It's got all sorts of sociological fallout like I'm getting into at Harrison; Spanish language growth. It could easily be a hybrid topic, good in the ag school as well as a liberal arts offering in sociology or another department.

"KSU's academic dean is looking for someone---ahem--- well versed with what's taking place. He wants someone to design and launch courses that could comprise a minor that grows into a major."

There was much to be considered at Kansas State, Mary added. In addition to a hefty raise to a healthy six-figure salary, she would have assistant professor status with full benefits and perks.

How did her name get on the Kansas State list? Apparently, a university administrator heard Mary deliver a paper at a conference and followed up with reading more of her work. Her courses would start as a hybrid, opening to students both in sociology and ag departments.

"Who knew?" said Mary. "I always figured those papers were so much dust in the wind. I never figured someone actually read them."

And the other job?

"You'll love this," she declared. "My alma mater. Arizona State. It's not anything concrete at this point, but my buddies in Tempe say there's going to be a bunch of openings announced later this year---some right up my alley. ASU's offering some early retirement packages. At least a half-dozen profs are expected to take them."

Mary didn't know what specific teaching slots would open. Too early for that. But---Wow!---Arizona State University. This was her homebase, where she earned her PhD and in the heart of Mexico border issues and initiatives that were her true love. Her---and my---home away from home in summers.

The ASU situation likely would not pay as much as KSU's, where potentially she also would take on administrative duties and be in position to create a department and serve as chair.

Lots to think about on the job front. No offers or official correspondence had taken place with ASU. She thought this would not happen until late in the first semester, when colleges traditionally like to finalize personnel lineups.

"Of course, you know what looms above everything?" I said. "Us."

"You're right. But nothing's getting solved in Whitey's tonight. Let's go home and sleep on it," Mary responded.

"Sounds good. Your bed or mine?"

"Yours. My bedroom's a mess."

Chapter 8

Starting Blocks

There were 14 of 15 present in Writing 1, so someone already dropped the course or had a good excuse for an absence. I hate it when students miss the first class in the new semester. With a waiting list of a half-dozen students, there was no problem filling any openings, but it typically meant lots of paperwork. I needed to get a quick handle on the missing student's status. If I did not hear from the absentee following the second class, I would automatically move someone up on the wait list. Hey! It's a jungle out there.

It's always good to hit the ground running. A fair amount of time in the first week is spent getting to know each other. You need to learn the students' likes, dislikes, and outlooks to better frame what to tackle during the semester. It can be a shocker for teachers when they learn a student can't name more than two U.S. presidents or never heard of typewriters.

More than anything I need to learn their writing abilities ASAP. Generally, I am disappointed. If it's really bad, which it occasionally is, we go back to pure basics. We become like the Nike advertisement: *"Just do it ...... and do it and do it."*

Then, we do it some more. Harrison has a writing laboratory, a walk-in clinic that students often walk-out of after a few sessions when they learn there's work and assignments.

I stress that writing is really reporting. First you gather details, then you use them. The more material you've gathered, the better the writing. It gives the writer options. "Think of it this way: You're building a brick house, and the more bricks you have, the more designs it leaves you."

And we use facts to illustrate the narrative, not opinions or conjecture. Hopefully this became evident with our first big effort for the local *Hoosier-Record:* A half-dozen stories Newt and I planned for my students to get published throughout the semester in his weekly newspaper.

There are informative stories that need to be written and run in a newspaper. Readers expect them and, it's the responsibility of a small-town newspaper to keep subscribers informed with needed information. Just the facts. Nothing fancy. No groundbreaking revelations. They can be advances of events, police blotter fodder, obituaries, and so on.

Bottom line: They don't require much creativity. They're about gathering details and reporting them in a responsible, helpful, and orderly manner. This is perfect for first-year students expecting the "great American novel" to flow from their fingertips.

Back-to-school stories fall in this category. Readers expect to learn and need to know when the doors open, faculty updates, bus schedules, lunch menus, new and important faces. This was a perfect opening for my writing class.

We could expand on what Newt, with little manpower, had mustered in recent years. At the same time, my students, paired into small teams for the assignment, get to see their names above a published piece. Nothing gets adrenalin flowing in this business like a little public recognition that is served up with a byline.

Right out of the box, here was the obvious. The *Hoosier-Record* traditionally kicks off the school year with an entire eight-page back-to-school pullout special section. It would carry our article on Page 1.

Newt was more than happy to get the added editorial help for this ready-made assignment. This year there would be a twist. In the past, the local public school system was all that was covered, but now he wanted Harrison College to be added to the mix.

"I probably would've done this in the past," he said. "but I could never be sure how much interest there was. Besides, to do it right, I barely had enough time with my schedule to cover the high school. This can't hurt."

Chapter 9

More Than a Teacher

In the few years I've been teaching I've learned students can regard you as some sort of personal counselor. A rapport builds beyond the classroom through independent projects or whatever.

Sometimes you listen to their woes---some serious, some not---and try to help find solutions. Most often this can be as simple as asking a professor for a letter of recommendation for grad school or a job.

Sometimes there are issues students simply do not want to discuss with parents. In these cases, they generally are on their own unless they find an empathetic faculty member or a friend. I've had a few of these situations in my short tenure at Harrison.

At one end of the spectrum, there was the coed---no names here---being stalked by an old boyfriend. For her, I helped navigate the process of obtaining a restraining order with the local county state's attorney.

One knock on the old boyfriend's door by a deputy sheriff and the problem evaporated. Quickly. He transferred to another school the next semester, never to be heard from again.

Then there was the Muslim student, one of only a few enrolled in our relatively milquetoast college. After a week's worth of unexplained absences, her knock on my office door was a bit of a surprise. It must have shown on my face.

"I'm so sorry to bother you with this," she said, "and I'm so sorry about my missed classes. But I don't know where else to turn. I enjoy your course so much and you seem so understanding. This isn't easy. I'd like to make my absences up somehow."

Her problem?

Fasting for Ramadan, a religious period that occurs for Muslims on the ninth month of the lunar-based Islamic calendar. The sacred rules call for abstinence from all food or drink, including water, from dawn to sunset.

And?

"I get so weak and dizzy from this," she explained. "Sometimes I can hardly stand up, let alone attend a class. This has been happening to me for so long. My parents do not understand. They do not even know I miss these classes. I don't want to see a doctor."

The student, close to tears, went on to explain that she figured this challenge would not qualify her for a medical excuse for her absences. Besides, just being a Muslim in full burka was enough challenge for her on our cliquish, clubby middle-class American campus.

She could always sense "that look" when she first interacted with other students, staff, or faculty. "If other students knew my religion was giving me a pass, this would not be good," she said.

Of all her professors, she sensed I would be most sympathetic. A softer touch, maybe? Flattered, but what to do?

In this case, my call to the registrar was not especially helpful. There was no policy covering absences due to fasting for religious reasons. End of conversation.

Instead, after looking over her class schedule, I called each of her profs. They, too, had been curious about her absences based on her otherwise excellent work. After hearing my explanation on her behalf, each was willing to accommodate with out-of-class assignments during Ramadan. End of problem.

Then there was this: A student with a dilemma that far exceeded the walls of my office. Joey Burke, a promising Writing 1 student. He was a "townie" of sorts, being from a tiny community several miles from campus.

Only a sophomore, Joey told me that he was pulling out of school just before classes started. His family had suffered a financial reversal that put his tuition out of reach---even if he lived at home, eliminated room and board, and commuted.

He came to me for a copy of my Writing 2 syllabus. He wanted to stay abreast in lieu of someday returning to Harrison classrooms. This was highly unusual. Joey told me that my course was the only one he liked enough to continue following. I was flattered.

"Sorry to learn of your situation, but I'll keep a light on for you," I said. This drew a faint smile. "Hopefully you'll be back soon."

There was a pause.

"Depends. My folks have been hit with some pretty big debt," Joey explained. "They haven't told me details, but their savings are blown and we may be losing our house and farm.

"My older sister is probably going to have to quit college, too. Purdue. She's closer to graduation. She might be able to scratch something out. Maybe transfer to Indiana U's branch over in Evansville. My mom's looking for some kind of job that pays more than being a cook at the high school.

"I got an older brother. Jimmy's kind of the family's ray of sunshine. He plays basketball at Lexington. He's a starter this year. A junior and plays guard, and has a full-ride athletic scholarship, so he's OK to stay in school.

"He worked a job this summer at a casino---the Duchess--- with a couple of teammates. Everyone's real proud of Jimmy."

I didn't wish to probe. After another awkward pause, Joey volunteered more.

"My family's broke, thanks to the Princess."

The what?

"The Princess. The casino boat. I don't know much about it, but I heard my mom and dad getting into a big shouting match one night. I guess Dad's been sneaking into the sportsbook, making lots of bets on football and basketball games. Losing most of 'em, too. I've got to get a full-time job to help out if we're going to keep our house."

Obviously, the newest feature on the casino boat, legalized wagering on sports events beyond horse racing and the usual gaming, was too much for Joey's father, Pete, to resist.

A big fan of major college basketball in general, and Indiana University in particular, Jimmy speculated his father had become hooked at the prospect of making a few bucks betting on games. Before legalized sports wagering he'd been on the boat only once in its ten years or so. Now he's found every excuse possible to be on board.

A prominent high school jock and (small) hometown hero himself, Joey's dad caught "the fever." No one could tell *him* how to pick winners and losers. He'd played the sports himself.

Quickly, Pete graduated from a social gambler to a problem gambler---apparently with no hope of becoming a successful gambler. He never would be smart enough to control his wagers, remain unemotional, and stay on the plus side. The slightest success simply was encouragement to raise the stakes.

In short, he was a perfect Princess customer.

Whether Indiana lost or won, Pete always thought he'd win with bets he placed---until he more often than not tore up the slip after another defeat. Soon, as the stakes grew and grew in his attempt to get ahead, the family piggy bank shrunk and shrunk. He had the fever.

The first hint to Joey there was a problem came with his dad's new interest in gambling odds published in the Evansville *Courier & Press*. Every morning he pored over them at the breakfast table. Then came the bombardment of TV advertising devoted to betting in the wake of the sellout to the activity by the NCAA and pro sports.

His mother never paid attention to family finances and therefore never noted their shrinking accounts. By the time Joey's dad came to his senses, he was almost $50,000--- $49,768 to be exact---in debt, mostly on his old and newly acquired credit cards.

Pete's competitive nature, combined with heightened stakes---sometimes reaching several thousand dollars per game, made him a perfect candidate for Gamblers Anonymous. "No way," he'd think to himself when he saw the GA literature scattered about the boat. That's for losers.

Chapter 10

Getting to Know You

The first few weeks in the front lines—otherwise known as the classroom---are always a crapshoot.

You need to get that early handle on the students. Appearances can be deceiving. The chatty ones often talk the talk, but don't walk the walk .... incapable of writing a complete paragraph but love to engage in name-dropping. At the same time, the quiet students off in the corner often have tons of pent-up potential. You need to find the plug to set it loose.

Then there are the nerds...the students who've mastered technology but come up short on social skills---like an inability to look you in the eye during a conversation or wearing socks that don't match.

No matter. Got to have them. They can design computer programs for anything, including creating stories by merely punching a few keys and, if all else fails, hacking their way into someone else's work.

Early on I learned to appreciate the techies. I'd start every new class with this: "Who's good with technology?" Inevitably several students raised their hands. "Good. Have a seat up close to me so I can lean on you for any assistance I need. I'm a content man, not systems."

This always drew a laugh. No problem. I learned early: Check my ego at the classroom door. Better to admit you don't know something than have the students discover it for themselves.

While I admit to being relatively new to college teaching, I mostly aim material and assignments toward better writers. I call it the "trickle down" theory. If I do not keep nudging and pushing at the top, I can lose the better students. And, at the same time, if I lower the bar, there is no guarantee the work resonates with poorer pupils.

Since I frequently call on students to voice observations, simple peer pressure can be a kind of second teacher in the room. More than anything, students don't like to sound stupid in front of classmates.

My ultimate goal for the semester is to have every student play a role in writing at least one article that appears in Newt's *Hoosier-Record*. To achieve this, I create two-person teams that share the story gathering and writing. A lot of mixing and matching goes into the process.

The students I put together need to complement each other to reach this goal. Ideally, at least one should be an able writer; the other needs to gather material, which in many cases, is the most important part.

Then, if I really get down and dirty, it's good to have a variety of cultural backgrounds represented in the mixes---city kids with farm kids, foreign students with local Harrison-ites, athletes with nerds, Hispanic, African American, cheerleader, whatever. I pick the teams and always try my best to create matchups with contrasting cultural backgrounds.

Harrison, with its southern Indiana location, Protestant roots, and small-town blend, isn't exactly Ellis Island. Still, in just a few years, my Writing 1 & 2 classes were creating buzz. Part of it was due to this *Hoosier-Record* link, and the students getting to see their work published for public consumption.

In the end, everyone learns, or should learn, that published writing in legitimate media doesn't get printed until it's been proofread and edited by someone other than the writer. No first drafts please. If it's a feature, finish it a day early and take a second look before making your deadline.

It is not unusual that the final copy for publication undergoes extensive editing. Tough on the egos, especially for any student whose writing went unchallenged before my class.

Both Newt and I gave close scrutiny to copy headed for the *Hoosier*. "Always remember your audience," Newt told my class, "and don't try to dazzle with your vocabulary. Pretend there's someone looking over your shoulder while you write."

Another key to any success had to be my, ahem, sometimes unconventional methods---or, as academics label it as experiential learning. The techniques are simple: Getting our hands dirty. As a student once told me, "Your class was kinda fun." I guess that was kinda complimentary.

There was buzz about starting a Harrison student newspaper. No way, or so I'd been advised by colleagues. I'd attended enough conferences attended by battle-scarred peers who'd been advisers.

"A landmine-ladened field," was one memorable observation from a peer at a comparable college. "You do nothing but put out fires. If it isn't dealing with pissed-off faculty bitching about how they were portrayed in a story, it's missed deadlines." The students ALWAYS wait until the last second to turn in stories.

There had once been a Harrison student newspaper that, during the Vietnam protest era, got dismantled by trustees when it was turned into "a protest rag sheet," according to one old-timer at a Rotary luncheon.

No matter. In my estimation, our *Hoosier-Record* arrangement was a better, more useful, and successful learning tool.

Several in this year's writing course took my literature course, and we already were familiar. "Can't get enough of you, professor," was how Tyvonia Braxton, a chatty, good-natured, third-year student put it. I was flattered by the presence of repeaters like her. I sort of regarded my other course, American Lit, as a bit of a snoozer.

In gregarious Tyvonia's case, she never met a stranger. A real ice-breaker. She was from upstate Gary and I was particularly glad to have her enrolled in my courses. The few papers she wrote for my American Literature course were excellent and, if published, would require little editing. She would make an easy transition into Writing 1 & 2, though it remained to be seen how she---or any of the students---would respond to having a partner on projects.

A few others showed promise: Arthur Graff, computer nerd from Bloomington (his father taught biology at Indiana U.); Dan Newman, a local from Harrison and on the football team; Karen Garner, a stylish writer from Valparaiso, and Donna Radtke, detail-oriented grind, Phi Beta Kappa-bound senior from Louisville.

In fact, it was easy to pigeon-hole students, something my teaching colleagues did routinely while overlooking the maturation process kids undergo in the four years (sometimes more) spent on campus. Today's wobbly, timid freshman can be tomorrow's captain of a champion Mock Trial team. Everything's a snapshot.

One student in this writing class was a definite puzzle to me, however. Craig Marshall. For a first-year Harrison student, Craig seemed old---in his mid-20s at least—and was extremely formal, occasionally calling me "sir" to the snickers of a few in the room. I looked forward to seeing his work, and any one-on-one, informal chats to get to know him better. Some of these kids have interesting back stories.

There are stories that need to be written and published in a newspaper. That definitely goes for the *Hoosier-Record,* too. Readers expect them and, it's the responsibility of a small-town newspaper to keep subscribers informed. Just the facts. Nothing fancy. No groundbreaking revelations. Small weeklies like Harrison's leave that to the wire services and big boys in Indianapolis and Louisville.

The meat and potatoes at our level are advances of events, police blotter fodder, obituaries, city council and school board business, car crashes and lunch menus. Bottom line: They don't require much creativity. It's about gathering details and reporting them in a responsible, helpful, and orderly manner. This is perfect for first-year students expecting the "great American novel" to flow from their fingertips.

Back-to-school stories fall in this category. Readers expect to learn and need to know when the doors open, faculty updates, bus schedules and lunch menus. This was a perfect opening for my writing class.

We could expand on what Newt, with scarce manpower, had mustered in recent years. Right out of the box, here was the obvious. The *Hoosier-Record* traditionally kicks off with an entire eight-page back-to-school pullout section, which would carry our article on Page 1 as the starting point for everything else in the special section.

Newt was more than happy to get the added editorial help for this ready-made assignment. This year there would be a twist. In the past, the local public school system was all that was covered, but now he wanted Harrison College to be added to the mix.

"I probably would've done this in the past," he said. "but I could never be sure how much interest there was. Besides, to do it right, I barely had enough time with my schedule to cover the high school. This can't hurt."

Here's the final effort from the two promising students I groomed for the assignment.

By Tyvonia Braxton
& Arthur Graff
Special to the Hoosier-Record

School bells have rung, ending the summer break, and attendance is up for both Harrison High School and Harrison College. This is especially significant, noted administrators at both schools due to drops in enrollment for the previous two years at both institutions.

"It's a very good sign," explained high school Supt. Warren Barr. "We think it shows growing confidence---and compliance---with pandemic guidelines." Added college president Jonathan Casey: "There's been a lot of scrambling the last two years, but obviously this shows a trust remains."

While the high school total is expected to fluctuate over the school year, the opening day enrollment of 579 students for grades 9-12 is a record high for the district.

The college enrollment is 1,350 students, approximately 125 over an average enrollment of the last two years. Perhaps more significant, said Casey, is a record number freshmen and transfers at 387.

Masks remain conditional at the high school, but quarantine mandates have been eased throughout the county's schools. They will be adjusted to meet appropriate standards.

"I'm proud of our district, considering what we've all been up against the last few years," said Barr. "If you just look at the facts, it's obvious masks and vaccinations are working. There is growing feeling of trust and comfort."

Harrison High School officials were ready for this year's growth, which saw an increase of 50 students over the district's *previous high mark. An increase in early enrollments and pre-school transfers were the tipoff.*

This meant the high school could finally get off to a relatively normal start with no last-minute scrambling of schedules and teacher assignments pending enrollment figures.

"We're getting closer and closer to 'normal,' whatever that is.," said Barr.

The high school campus, building and facilities look totally familiar to returning students. The school board, uncertain because of the Covid-19 pandemic, put all major infrastructure projects on hold two years ago. Board members are expected to take a second look at needs in upcoming meetings.

There is also talk of joint programming with Harrison College, which would be a first in the long histories of both institutions. This could include shared use of facilities---the college has a swimming pool, the high school doesn't---and academic programs in which high school students can take appropriate courses that would transfer into college credit. In addition, the college is known to be considering tuition discounts for residents of Indiana.

"For now, we're basically in a position of addressing almost all shortcomings as they pop up," declared board president Julia Meade. "We just need a good year of normalcy."

The last major, infrastructure project was completed in 2018, when Thomas Auditorium was completed. In addition to its use as an athletic arena, it could quickly be transitioned into a performing arts center. Less obvious, but just as important, has been upgrading of the school's classroom technology equipment and programs.

"We couldn't have timed those (tech) improvements any better," said Meade. "They gave us much better reach with students when we were heavy into distance learning."

There will be a significant number of new faces in the teaching and staff ranks. There are nine new teachers (individual biographies can be found on Page 2A of this special section). This is a higher number than usual with pandemic-related conditions the alleged catalyst.

The highest-profile newcomer will be the principal, James Rowan. He comes to Harrison from Speedway High School in the Indianapolis suburbs, where he was an assistant principal for three years. He is a graduate of DePauw University with a master's degree in education from Morehead State University in Kentucky.

The college's academic year also started with no, new major facilities to greet incoming students, but it's not much of a secret this is expected to change. A major capital drive is being organized for building a new science and technology center.

"It's nothing official," said Casey. "On the other hand, it is our intention to ramp up our involvement to always remain current while paying respect to the traditional disciplines."

The president acknowledged also that the college will be looking into future areas of mutual bonding with the high school and other parts of the Harrison community.

"It makes all the sense in the world," he said. "After all, we are neighbors with much to share."

Chapter 11

Soldiering On

In addition to a back-to-school story effort, another *Hoosier-Record* staple focused on Veterans Day (Nov. 11). Newt anointed my class for an article to be part of a special four-page memorial section. The section would be county-wide in scope and plenty of bountiful advertising, of course.

This newspaper package, though smaller than the back-to-school section, had become especially popular with readers. Several years ago Newt added a new wrinkle to hike its profile: He published the name of every county resident who served in the armed forces. Ever. This took up a full page and the initial search was a painstaking effort.

Newt dug up names dating all the way back to the Civil War. Several veterans were mistakenly left out in the first years, drawing complaints. He took a lot of razzing from several Rotary Club luncheon tablemates when they were among the missing. The fact that he dug up a few names of Confederate soldiers also raised a few eyebrows, but he didn't flinch.

"Lots of work to put that baby together," he said. "My eyes got pretty bleary going through the newspaper files, county records and such. I got a few volunteers---retired guys from the

American Legion Post here---to help. Worth it, though. Our circulation got a nice bump."

Last year, no griping apparently meant the list finally was complete---though new residents had to be closely monitored for additions. Harrison had an interesting military history, one that provided surprises from years past. Not exactly full of political correctness either.

For starters, William Henry Harrison, the U.S. president and namesake for our county, community and college, made his bones leading military forces killing indigenous Native Americans to make it easier for settlers to steal their land for American expansion.

Later in the Civil War, there was plenty of Confederate sympathy in this southern Indiana region to counter the state's official standing as Union. After all, the bordering Ohio River served as the Mason-Dixon boundary. Several small, undocumented skirmishes took place on the Indiana side and the Harrison community itself was known to have provided at least a dozen or so rebel army volunteers.

"I caught some flak when I included them on my local veterans' list," said Newt. "That's OK. Taking heat comes with the job. I did misspell several names, though. In my book, that was a real sin."

There were several ongoing Civil War mysteries in the county never solved, too. My students perked up at hearing that potential challenge. Last year's class had gained a reputation for sleuthing when it unraveled a 50-year-old local murder mystery.

"When do we get to do something like they did?" asked one of my students in our very first meeting.

"Hold your horses," was my generation-bending response--- a response needing explanation when it was met by blank stares. "Believe it or not, some of you are not capable at this point to write something for a public audience."

One mystery that had some potential: Several homes in the county were underground railroad stops for runaway slaves. This narrative gained steam several years ago when the best-selling book, "The Underground Railroad," by Colson White-head, made the rounds. Did the structures still exist in southern Indiana with relevant---and possibly valuable---artifacts?

The other immediate possibility was that somewhere in the county a small, secret, and abandoned cemetery existed with graves of local Confederate Army enlistees and supporters. Did the inhabitants prefer their own cemetery, or were they banned from Harrison's public cemetery on the edge of town for being traitorous?

Good possibilities for the future for my writing students to pursue? There probably was not enough time in the semester to mount a chase. I wanted to leave nothing undone by the semester's end. Perhaps this would be a good Independent Study project for students who develop real reportorial chops. These would be nice coups for the *Hoosier-Record*, similar to a half-century old unraveled cold case article.

There's always a story behind the story. It can play out in different ways, and though they didn't know it, there was a simmering issue behind our Veterans Day advance story. Newt and I decided it was too hot for the students to handle at this stage in their development. Trust had to be earned.

The backstory revolved around the Harrison American Legion Post's upcoming Veterans Day keynote speaker, Margaret (Margie) Kroll, who would be the first woman to deliver the event's speech.

Hard to believe this deep into the 21st Century, but there were some on the program's selection committee vehemently opposed to having Margaret, a woman, as keynoter. There was no discernable, objectionable reason except that she was a female, a first for this important community gathering and, as we know, the first rime can aways be painful.

Incredibly the American Legion committee vote was 5-4, with Jim Baker, a Desert Storm vet still active in the Army Reserves but now living in Iowa, the runner-up speaker candidate.

My feeling, if asked, was that the students were not seasoned enough to tackle a community-wide gender dispute. In fact, nobody except committee members and a few others even knew of the background tension.

In the end, the best part of this saga for my class was timing. When the November 11 holiday rolled around, it was deep into the college's first semester giving my assigned students plenty of time. They, as well as Margaret, the speaker, were never aware of the friction.

Here was the final Veterans Day piece put together by the students:

By Lauren Dill
& Jorge Lopes
Special to the Hoosier-Record

Veterans Day ceremonies this year will have a familiar look in many ways.

There will be Harrison community's traditional parade, led by flag-bearing American Legion Abraham Lincoln Post 212 honorary officers representing every major U.S. conflict starting with the Korean War of the 1950s---but sadly missing Lucian Zimmer, the county's remaining World War II representative who passed earlier this year.

In addition, there will be a half-dozen registered floats, at least ten classic cars at last count, assorted sign-carrying Boy Scout and Girl Scout troops, special interest organizations such as the local historical preservation society, government office holders, fire trucks and ambulances from Harrison and Liberty.

Music? There will be lots of that, starting with marching bands from the county's two high schools---Harrison and Liberty. And the Evansville Marching Emeralds Drum & Bugle Corps will strut after a two-year absence.

"We'd like to think this year's parade will be a knockout... our vets deserve the recognition," said Bob Mohn, commander of the local American Legion Post. "I know we worked very hard putting this together. It's one of the biggest highlights on our yearly calendar. I'm very proud to play a part."

Everyone assembles at the Harrison High School athletic fields. Marchers step off promptly at 10 a.m. with a blast from the community's central alarm siren. The traditional, mile-long route passes through downtown before ending at the cemetery on the north edge of town.

There, with U.S. flags traditionally adorning every veteran's grave, followers will witness something different with this long-standing event---Margaret (Margie) Kroll will become the first female veteran to deliver the keynote address from the gazebo overlooking graves. Her speech, "A Better World," will follow Harrison Senior Class President Eugene Young's delivery of Abraham Lincoln's famous "Gettysburg Address."

"It's a great honor to have Margie as our featured speaker," said Mohn. "I know she'll do a wonderful job. We're very proud of her. She's always been very supportive of the work we do at the Abraham Lincoln Post."

Many are familiar with Kroll's decades long career as the chief nurse at Harrison Memorial Hospital. Not so many are familiar with this: As a U.S. Army nurse, she was one of approximately 11,000 women who volunteered to serve in Vietnam on medical duty.

"I was young and just out of nursing school," she said. "It (enlisting, serving) just seemed like the thing to do."

Furthermore, the use of helicopters between battle zones and first aid stations meant wounded soldiers often were treated within a half-hour of combat. Twelve-hour shifts (six days per week) often became 24-hour shifts.

"Yes, I saw things no person should have to see," she said. "Nothing can compare to that experience."

Many nurses, like Margaret, also did volunteer social work with Vietnamese residents in their villages. While serving abroad, she was promoted from 1st Lieutenant to Captain. She was awarded several medals for her service. "It wasn't M.A.S.H.," she said. "It was real life and death."

Margaret was the first woman to become a member of American Legion Abraham Lincoln Post 212. She has served in several leadership roles.

"I'm honored to be the speaker," she said, "but I deplore that anyone should have to go through, or even witness, a war like Vietnam to be part of their life at this point."

The event at the cemetery will conclude with a lone trumpeter, Harrison High School senior Steve Harris, playing "Taps."

Chapter 12

Marshall's Plan

That Veterans Day advance story my students did for the *Hoosier-Record?* It was Page One in an issue first available on Thursday evening. Friday morning at 9 a.m. there was forceful knock on my Durham Hall office door.

"Got a few minutes," asked Craig Marshall, my stoic, ultra-polite Writing 1 student. His large frame took up most of the doorway. We were an hour from our class meeting.

"The Vets Day story got me thinking," he said. "I've got something I'd like to ask. Hopefully I'm not out of line."

"Come in, have a seat. I've always got time for a chat with a student though we'll have to hustle." Five minutes into our unscheduled session I wished there'd been more time, like several hours. Craig's story was interesting.

It turns out he was discharged from the U.S. Army only a month before Harrison classes started. He hustled to enroll with the help of several veteran-support groups and govern-ment-promised scholarships.

He'd been in college---University of Lexington in Ken-tucky---for a year before dropping out and enlisting.

"Lost," he explained, of this earlier experience. "Didn't really know what I was doing in college then. Enlisting seemed to be the thing to do and stop wasting time and money. I was spending more time in bars than the library.

"Lexington will do that to you, and I came from a big family. They couldn't really afford much, let alone me wasting my time and their money."

Craig was from Owensboro, Kentucky, on the Ohio River halfway between Evansville and Louisville. To cut down expenses following his discharge, he moved in with his parents for the first semester, found a weekend job, and commuted an hour to Harrison College for weekday classes.

"Not a bad setup for now," he said. "I knew I didn't want to go back to Lexington. Too many temptations. I was a little wary enrolling at a small, private four-year school like Harrison. It's growing on me. It takes a while to get used to being older than everyone in your class."

"Except me?" This drew a subtle laugh, and an apology for addressing me as "sir" in the classroom. "At least you didn't salute," was my response.

With only a year of college under his belt, it was made clear to him that his rank as a sergeant was as far as he would advance in the military. He needed a degree to get into officer training programs.

"If I had it to do over again, I would've gotten into some sort of ROTC program at the very start at Lexington. Would've paid for my college, too. Now it's basically too late. At my age, the Army's only going to be interested if I could get into graduate school, which I can't without a degree."

Turns out that Craig, even if he'd advanced as far as he could in rank, accumulated some great skills that already made him valuable. Mainly, it was his technology talents. They made him extremely useful to officers above him, which, in turn, made them look good.

Soon he was transferred to an intelligence office, where he became a force in content data entry. At one point, this included unraveling the U.S.'s botched exit from Hamad Karzai International Airport in Kabul, Afghanistan.

"I did two tours over there before that," he said. "All my work on the airport disaster took place on the receiving end in the States. I can't talk about it. Let's just say that I may have a future in logistics."

Craig's plan now was to take as little time as possible getting that bachelor's degree. Then, he'd see if the Army would be interested enough to let him re-enlist and support him in a graduate program---his path to becoming an officer.

"If not the Army, there's always the Marines," he added, with a laugh.

His strategy was to stack up credit hours at Harrison---summer schools and full loads---as quickly as possible. "I did some math," he said. "I could probably get it done and graduate in two-and-half years. One thing would help a lot."

And that was? "Those Independent Study projects you put together. In reading the college's catalog, I noticed a student can have up to eight hours of credit included in their total with supervised projects outside the classroom."

Harrison's limit was 16 hours of credit per semester. However, students were allowed an extra four per term---twice---for an independent project under a professor's guidance. It had to be approved by a special academic committee, a process I was familiar with---something I had done to get my students credit for outside work with the *Hoosier-Record.*

In Craig's case, I told him there was a problem. "I'd be willing to work with you on this, but I have no understanding of your capabilities. Independent Study is for good students with lots of self-discipline. In the past, I've always had a good handle on the participants. Trust is a big part of it. I've yet to see enough of your work, though I certainly appreciate---at this point---your ambitions."

Craig understood. I had to think discipline, based on his military service, would not be a problem. But I did need more samples of his work---and we agreed to meet on this later in the term. It would not be too late for the second semester.

Chapter 13

His Last Stand

Craig Marshall spent little time getting back to me pitching a *Hoosier-Record* story idea to be considered. At first glance, I knew his story would be an instant winner with readers. This was rare for a student. Generally, I had to do the thinking when it came to realistic ideas that matched our newspaper audience as well as my students' capabilities.

Newt agreed with my assessment of Craig's pitch, tossing in a few suggestions of his own. After all, it was his newspaper. My only condition to Craig was that he take on a classmate as a project partner. Collaboration. This was my rule for all the stories headed for the presses. Not only was it a good way to spread learning, but it also helped boost morale for students to see their name above the article.

Here was the finished project:

By Karen Garner
& Craig Marshall
Special to The Hoosier-Record

Diamond City, Ind.---Located just five miles north of Harrison, this collection of a half-dozen or so homes punctuated with a convenience store and auto repair shop is so small it does not have its own zip code. The grammar school closed so long ago there's there are not enough living alums to have reunions.

There is an intersection for County Road 2 in the middle of this dot of a community, and for anyone turning eastward on the gravel County Road CC there is one last sight of long-ago habitation of a town called Diamond City: An abandoned church with a small cemetery barely visible from the road. The tombstones are buried in unruly shrubbery, grass, and weeds that, at the most, get trimmed twice a year by the Harrison County maintenance department.

Too bad. The cemetery is the final resting place for a survivor of, arguably, one of America's most famous massacres: Custer's Last Stand. His name is Jimmy O'Brien, born in Ireland sometime in the 1850s and died in 1919 on a potato farm in southern Indiana, not far from his grave. There is nothing to acknowledge Jimmy's involvement with George Armstrong Custer's ill-fated 7th U.S. Army Calvary detachment.

He had emigrated to the U.S. in 1870, lived briefly in New York City, and, in his search for employment, found his way to Chicago. It was in the Windy City where he enlisted and spent nearly 20 years in the U.S. Army.

As a member of the 7th Army, Jimmy spent much of that run with Custer engaged in the Great Sioux Wars of the Great Plains. This included June 5-6 in Montana in 1876, when the famous annihilation of Custer and everyone in his 700-member force was slaughtered.

But not Jimmy O'Brien.

Instead, as Custer's regiment was leaving camp on the fateful day, according to U.S. War College documents, he was one of three members ordered at the last minute to join a different group to help fill its ranks---miles away from the battlefield and unaware the subsequent massacre was unfolding.

O'Brien did not entirely escape medical treatment as a soldier, however. He was wounded twice in subsequent, bloody skirmishes with the Sioux before eventually being transferred from the Indian Wars of the west. His assignments as an Army sergeant then took him to a variety of locations in the U.S.

He was with a unit ready to enter the Spanish-American War. Then stationed at historic Fort Sheridan in the Chicago suburbs, he retired from active duty to find work in a local hospital. There he met and married a nurse, Anna Dooley, and eventually moved to southern Indiana to help work her parents' farm. He also served as a volunteer fireman in the nearby community of Lexington, according to newspaper notices, and rose to the rank of chief.

He died In 1919 a victim of the Spanish Flu epidemic. The funeral was in the still-standing---but abandoned---Diamond City Baptist Church not far from his in-law's farm. He was buried in the adjacent cemetery, where his tombstone gives scant indication of his historic military service.

The story drew much praise. *Hoosier-Record* contributions to the publication from my class were gaining an audience. More important the features filled a nice gap, providing more information in a well-written fashion.

Just as gratifying to me was finding in Craig another student---not that much younger than me---whose work was mature and capable. I was pretty sure we could "do some business" on Independent Study projects.

"Karen was a big help on this, especially with smoothing out the writing," he said. "Not my call, but I could easily work with her again. It was huge that she's a local from the Harrison area. She knew her way around. Kept us from wasting time and energy."

And the military details? Just how did you come by all that good background stuff?

"Well," said Craig, following a lengthy pause, "don't forget I was in the Army."

And?

"I spent a couple years in Intelligence," he said. "This gave me a lot of access to records and archives and those sorts of documented Army details."

As he saw my eyebrows start to raise, he quickly added: "nothing illegal, though. Every source was public record, though I'm pretty sure the general public would have trouble knowing where to find things I did."

I left it at that, though I did eventually get a call about the story that pleased me as much as anything. It was Bob Mohn, commander of the local Abraham Lincoln American Legion Post. He was so taken by the article that he was going to gather volunteers to go to the Rochester cemetery for clean-up duty.

"We're going to make it a regular thing, probably monthly," he said. "I'm going to find if there are any more vets buried there, and we'll put American flags on their graves every patriotic holiday."

Newt couldn't have been happier after hearing that news. "You know you're doing OK when a story moves people to take action, positive action."

Chapter 14

Land of Lincoln?

Illinois calls itself the Land of Lincoln. It says so on the state's license plates.

Furthermore, the 16th president of the United States is buried in Illinois and his official library and museum are in the state's capitol, Springfield. In 2019, the last full year before the Pandemic, close to a quarter million visitors took in those facilities.

And where does Indiana, the neighbor, fit into this? Well, the Hoosier state wasn't exactly a bus stop for Honest Abe.

Lincoln spent important formative years in Indiana. It was where he learned to read and write, got his first job, and was exposed to the outside world working on riverboats. He visited exotic crossroads such as New Orleans and became aware of slavery, witnessing a slave auction on one of his Mississippi River trips.

Indiana residents point out gladly that he didn't move to Illinois until he turned 21, having spent 14 years in Indiana obtaining his piecemeal education. The six men from the Hoosier state who became vice-presidents---among them Dan Quayle and Mike Pence---are no substitute for one Honest Abe when it comes to tourist attractions.

You can find memorials dedicated to the Great Rail Splitter---another then-important skill (rail splitting) he learned in Indiana---scattered throughout his Indiana roots.

And while Illinois may get more visitors and tourism revenue from his legacy, there is also a quiet, relative unknown, lucrative cottage industry in Honest Abe's Indiana wake. Collectibles. This is mostly a cash business that, if reported to Uncle Sam, would rank as one of the state's leading products.

Much of the memorabilia---or "Lincolnalia," as collectors call it---gets moved through big auction houses, but for alert and savvy treasure hunters, there are plenty of gems to be found in small gift shops, rummage sales and bookstores that dot towns in the state's bottom half---Harrison, Boonville, Dale, Ferdinand, and others.

"The thing is," explained Carl Soggenheim, a Lincoln expert and Rotary Club luncheon program speaker, "he traveled all over the East Coast during his presidency and left a huge paper trail. But rarely did he make a trip west of Pennsylvania during the Civil War. His Indiana years are still relatively unplowed.

"His assassination alone was big for collectors... locks of his hair ($7,500), personal etchings ($24,500) fragments of his skull taken by surgeons who worked on him, wallpaper strips from the room in which he died," continued Soggenheim. "Hell, his stove pipe hat from the night he was shot once sold for nearly two-million dollars. And don't forget things like his autograph on a hand-written copy of the Gettysburg Address ($3.1 million).

"Now all that has left the Midwest, fertile territory for stuff---if it can be identified. The items have to be rare if they're from Indiana.

"The trouble is that Lincoln was brought up in pretty rustic conditions. Nothing against Indiana, but there wasn't much documentation in this state then. If it's from Indiana and got an Abe connection, it's likely got some real value. No one knows exactly what they're looking for, but that doesn't stop anyone from looking. Certainly not me.

"We do know he spent a lot of time as a youngster right here in Harrison County."

On any given weekend, these collectible hunters are the out-of-town strangers seen scrutinizing informal garage and rummage sales as well as flea markets. They pull up in their car (typically with out-of-state plates), head straight to books and framed materials, and do a quick perusal.

Quietly and without drawing attention they take pictures of items with cameras equipped with special software that identifies provenance and values. You never know what households unknowingly will toss out valuable pieces of memorabilia passed down through several, unknowing generations.

Soggenheim knows the drill. He retired from a high school teaching position in Louisville to pursue his Lincoln interests on a full-time basis. Most of his revenue comes from eBay transactions, but when he hits on something with potentially large value, he's established his own surreptitious pipeline to big-time auction houses. He also runs a small antique and bookstore in Evansville.

"I convinced myself there's gold in them thar' hills, believe me," he joked with our club, "and it cost me a marriage when I quit teaching to look for it. My wife thought I was nuts. Well, Lincoln is hot in the memorabilia world. You don't hear much about it, and that's just the way collectors want it."

What started as a hobby for him quickly evolved into a business with this find at a garage sale: A musket used by explorer George Rogers Clark, a Revolutionary War hero and one-half of the legendary Lewis & Clark team that trekked to Oregon. The firearm---he used it on the historic adventure---is on display in Vincennes, Indiana, where a national park and museum was dedicated in Clark's honor.

Following an exhaustive vetting, he got it certified as the "real deal." He sold it to a wealthy East Coast collector for a reported $200,000. Officially, it is "on loan" to the museum in Vincennes. The windfall allowed him to quit his high school teaching job in Evansville to open a small antique shop and deal in antiquities on a full-time basis.

He was a popular guest speaker at Rotary luncheons in Indiana. His special expertise was Abraham Lincoln's years in the state.

"People forget," he liked to remind, "that Lincoln spent 14 very formative years in Indiana. Many things became public record after he moved and got elected president. He left a trail of lower profile, but no less significant, artifacts in Indiana. They're just more difficult to document. When you can, the location adds to their value."

Lincoln's stovepipe hats, written and signed copies of his speeches, a lock of hair, or anything he was wearing on the evening he was shot in Ford's Theatre have been big ticket items. His eyeglasses alone once went for $250,000 in an auction. In the same sale, a topcoat cost one happy collector $400,000 and another shelled out $175,000 for his wallet.

Where does the Lincoln rainbow lead these days, Soggenheim was asked at the Rotary luncheon. Where's the Lincolnalia pot of gold?

"Books," he answered, without the slightest pause. "Abe didn't read his first book until he was eleven or twelve while living in Indiana---and, even then, there were only a half-dozen or so he had access to. We have a good idea what they were, but nobody's sure they still exist. But that doesn't stop anyone from looking. They'd be worth a mint."

At the top of the list? That would be the book first published in 1800 titled *"The Life of Washington"* by Parson Weems. At age 11 or 12, historians mostly agree this was Abe's first read.

Museums and rich collectors would pay plenty to get it---easily in the mid-six figures. Its value would be enhanced as something important from Lincoln's years in Indiana, where precious little memorabilia existed or was gobbled up by the official Lincoln Library and Museum in Illinois.

Weems was way ahead of his time as a marketer. He died in 1825, but his books continued to be published after his passing. There was no way to tell what year the edition read by Lincoln was printed or, for that matter, if Lincoln's copy still existed. Supposedly, his copy contains scribbled notes by the future U.S. president. His distinctive handwriting would be the sure giveaway.

The George Washington biography also was the first to forward the apocryphal tale of little George chopping down a cherry tree that led to his "I cannot tell a lie" confession.

It read like this:

When George was about six years old, he was made the wealthy master of a hatchet, *of which, like most little boys, he was immoderately fond of, and was constantly going about chopping everything that came in his way.*

One day, in the garden, where he often amused himself hacking his mother's pea sticks, he unluckily *tried the edge of his hatchet on the body of a beautiful young English cherry tree, which he barked so terribly, that I don't believe the tree ever got the better of it.*

The next morning the old gentleman finding out what had befallen his tree, which, by the by, was a great favorite, came into the house, and with much warmth asked for the mischievous author, declaring at the same time, that he would not have taken five guineas for his tree. Nobody could tell him anything about it.

Presently George and his hatchet made their appearance. George, said his father, do you know who killed that beautiful little cherry tree yonder in the garden? This was a tough question, and George staggered under it for a moment; but quickly recovered himself: and looking at his father, with the sweet face of youth brightened with the inexpressible charm of all-conquering truth, he bravely called out, I can't tell a lie, Pa; you know I can't tell a lie. I did cut it with my hatchet.

Run to my arms, you dearest boy, cried his father in transports, run to my arms; glad am I, George, that you killed my tree; for you have paid me for it a thousandfold. Such an act of heroism in my son, is more worth than a thousand trees, though blossomed with silver, and their fruits of purest gold.

Any museum would be thrilled to have the book. None more than the Indiana Historical Society, but they'd have to stand in line. As far as anyone knew, it was "in play" ---it could pop up anywhere.

There were other Weems' books that quite possibly were among Lincoln's early reads. They included *Benjamin Franklin's Autobiography, Robinson Crusoe,* and *The Arabian Nights.*

Why else was the Washington book so special? In addition to being considered the very first book Lincoln read, it supposedly contained notes scribbled by Abe. Nobody knew for sure, since there had been only one known sighting of the book two generations before it disappeared into someone's personal library, attic, basement or, hopefully not, trash bin.

Soggenheim said the Evansville library's used book sale is a must-attend event for him. As the largest public library in southern Indiana and northern Kentucky, the annual event draws several thousand patrons. You never know what might be found in the stacks of a used book sale, especially this one. For sure, anything related to Abe gets snatched quicker than a Grisham or Sandford, he added with a smirk.

As soon as the Rotary meeting was adjourned, Newt and I quickly agreed my students couldn't miss with something about Honest Abe, an occasional visitor to Harrison in his lifetime. A subsequent check in *Hoosier-Record* files showed precious little published on any visits but lots of possibilities.

Yes, it could be a nice change of pace. Learn some history while compiling a story. I put it on my list.

Chapter 15

School Daze

Our earliest stories published in the *Hoosier-Record*---a back-to-school roundup, Veterans Day celebration---were standard fare for local newspapers. Since they were part of special sections, they could be counted on to produce much sought after revenue.

We needed to continue to hit the road, like Craig Marshall did with the "Custer Survivor" piece. Start snooping for more colorful features. Give readers something interesting and unexpected about their home base, something they wouldn't know if the paper hadn't printed it.

Furthermore, Newt said the stories did not even have to be in Harrison or Harrison County as long as they were in southern Indiana. We could break free. Southern Indiana had a noteworthy, but unknown, history for most readers.

To set an example, and following a little research on my part, I assigned this historic travel piece to two students I figured to be both creative and accurate. We loaded their writing with pictures, old and new, found in *Hoosier-Record* files.

By Daniel Newman
& Selma Forbes

Special to the Hoosier-Record

*New Monroe, Ind.---It is difficult to believe this tiny Ohio River town of 150 residents in Harrison County once was an en-*tertainment capital *for southern Indiana. In fact, it is difficult to believe this community, now with less than 100 residents, was a community at all.*

Located at the end of County Road 6, cars do not exactly whisk by this blip on the map. If they did, they'd end up in the old Ohio as the pothole laden road ends shortly before the river's shoreline.

Has New Monroe seen better days? There had to be a few. Somewhere, somehow.

The town, second oldest in Indiana, was laid out in 1815. And most likely, its many good times in its 200-plus year history took place in the Monroe Opera House built in 1854.

That's when the community was entering its then-glory years as an overnight port stop for a huge stream of riverboat traffic. The line of horse-drawn wagons, would often stretch for a mile while waiting for goods to be loaded or unloaded.

The town swelled to a population of several thousand residents in the late 1800s and early 1900s. It bustled with river-oriented commerce, according to its long-defunct newspaper, the New Monroe Times.

And those important business interests of the day came with diversions---a racetrack, saloons, several hotels, casinos, and the New Monroe Opera House. The great Dan Patch standard-bred racehorse, a world-famous, record-setting pacer, drew thousands just to see it do several laps in a special exhibition

In its Heyday, the opera house drew popular, traveling acts that worked the Upper Midwest circuit. From individuals like Lillian Russell and the Ray Charles of that era, pianist Blind Boone, to groups such as Emma Abbott's English Opera Company and

The New Orleans Grand Colored Concert Company, few troupes bypassed this venue. Many arrived by boat.

And there's significant speculation that past and present residents love to consider: was a youthful Abraham Lincoln ever in an audience for a production? He was raised only a few miles away and worked on riverboats making deliveries up and down the Ohio and nearby Mississippi Rivers that docked here.

Maybe a curious Abe did visit, but it's more likely his assassin, John Wilkes Booth, or brothers Edwin and Junius Booth, performed there as thespians---possibly with Abe in the audience!

The Booths were prominent actors of the pre-Civil War era, making the rounds with traveling productions that didn't miss many popular venues in the Midwest. There's no record of this in the New Monroe Times.

"A community had to be large enough to support an opera house if it was being built only for live entertainment," said Russell Wilson, chief archivist for the Indiana Historic Preservation Society. "These were the places to go to see a play or a musical review or whatever was popular on stage at the time."

He added, "The New Monroe Opera House with its seating (500) was a biggie, and very popular because of its location."

Today, the once busy New Monroe business district consists of a gas station, mini-mart, post office, and about a half-dozen shuttered and decrepit abandoned buildings. Still standing is the opera house, propped up inside by makeshift poles and circled outside by a ten-foot-high wire fence. Demolition appears a certainty.

For many, this opera house scenario may sound familiar. Indiana preservation experts estimate there are at least 200 of these entertainment relics, vacant or re-purposed, still standing in the state. There is at least one in every county. Those with landmark status, like the one in New Monroe, will remain in place though badly in need of repair.

The theater artifacts---scenery, posters, programs, seats, stage lights and such---have long disappeared as highly-regarded collectibles. However, two years ago, noted Wilson, several items from the house got showcased by a collector on Public Broadcasting's Antiques Road Show.

"I would love to have had a closer look at those items," he said. "The bottom line is that, unknown to many, there is a very brisk, lucrative market for historical artifacts in southern Indiana. A lot of important history occurred in this state. It included New Monroe."

Twenty-five years ago, an investment group---one that owned several casinos on the Ohio River---took a close look at locating a fourth riverboat here, the Princess. This would've produced a windfall for the tiny town with its complementary businesses and parking on the shore.

Not only did Bel-Tar Gaming decide to take a pass on New Monroe, many locals felt it rubbed salt in the wound by locating in an unincorporated patch a mile upstream across the county line. They took advantage of improved tax benefits and a barrel full of additional incentives.

That county, Mercer, got an added boost when gambling on sporting events, or sports books, subsequently became legal. This meant millions more into county coffers---and left New Monroe empty-handed.

Chapter 16

Homework 101

My writing class was having a nice run. The stories published in the *Hoosier-Record,* though mostly local focus, made for solid reading. Newt was getting good responses. All our pieces prompted letters to the editor.

Just as important: They were responsible for a small circulation uptick, according to Newt's figures. I know that four students in this class told me their parents had taken out subscriptions to make sure they didn't miss any of their progeny's work---and three were out-of-state (Illinois, Ohio, Florida).

For Danny Newman, one especially promising, chatty student, it was his grandparents in Florida who started reading the *Hoosier-Record* as subscribers. They lived in Naples. "My Grandpa said he always liked the 'feel' of a newspaper in his hands. He said he could always find something of interest --- even if it was a crossword puzzle or obituary---in a paper."

At the very least, the newspaper gave these first-time subscribers a feel for their offspring's new environment. The majority of the Harrison College student body was from Indiana, but, as just about anyone can tell you, the far southern, rural region of the state was an acquired taste---even for those from the top half of the state above Interstate 70.

My favorite exercise that I mentioned earlier was to divide the class into small teams. This was a good way to add context to their work.

A first-generation Hispanic, Jorge Lopes, from Arizona, teamed with Lauren Dill someone from an affluent family from on Chicago's toney North Shore. Jorge, fluent in Spanish and whose parents were immigrants from Mexico City, made it possible to add depth to a feature piece on Harrison's only truly ethnic restaurant---El Pulpo Loco with Mexican fare---unless you considered Domino's as Italian.

Or how about the African American Tyvonia Braxton, daughter of a pastor in upstate Gary's inner city with a farm kid, George Kirkpatrick, from rural Indiana?

"Did you know there was a turkey processing factory close by where a lot of the local people work?" Tyvonia told me after class one day. "Turkeys? Who knew? Where I come from everyone works in steel mills."

Then there was Tao Wang and Kevin Simpson. Tao was part of Harrison's exchange program with Xiamen University in China. Kevin, a jock, was the backup quarterback and in line to be the school's starter next season.

A final writing project was a status report on President Casey's effort to start an eSport program. Their story was a mindblower for many readers, most of whom had no idea hundreds of colleges competed against each other in video gaming. Furthermore, if the president had his way, there would be related eSport courses.

"I think it was a perfect story for us to do," Kevin Simpson told me after their work crossed my desk late in the semester. "I love to compete. Tao's a whiz with technology." The story drew a half-dozen letters to the editor in the *Hoosier-Record*. All but one expressed shock at learning tuition dollars could be spent on video gaming.

Some of my knee-jerk faculty peers thought I was unduly fostering a culture clash with my "team concept" pedagogy. My response always was: "And your point is?"

The writing course met three times per week, and a big chunk of at least one weekly session was devoted solely to story ideas. How do you find them? Does it provide information previously unknown to the reader? What are their ingredients? Do they match the paper's readership?

Always, always think local first, of course. Give readers something entertaining and informative they are not likely to read in another publication or view on television or social media. This was a stretch for some students.

"Craig Marshall's story about Custer's last stand survivors buried in the county was a great model," was my perfect illustration. "He fed a local angle---known by practically no one---to an otherwise well-known piece of history."

With that, Craig promptly stood up and saluted. This drew a big laugh. By now everyone knew his military background. Nothing like a little humor to get the students' attention, especially if it was a professor's lame, dated joke.

"Think about it," I continued. "Southern Indiana is overrun with historic material---Lincoln, Civil War tensions, Underground Railroad, and the Ohio River. And that's just in a few decades. You just need to dig through old newspapers. Some of the best stuff work students have done for me was some form of history. The best stories often are behind us, not in front.

"Craig, I'm guessing you and your teammate (Karen Garner) spent a lot of time in research before coming up with that beauty---a Custer survivor buried here under our noses."

Craig, with a nod toward Karen, answered: "Not exactly. I overheard two old-timers talking about it while standing in line at a convenience store out on the highway."

Sometimes a little luck helped.

My system did have this boost for some: Students would propose an idea to me a day or so before an appointed 'idea discussion' class, and then I'd pick 5 or 6 suggestions to be inspected by everyone. Purposely, the identity of the contributor would be left out of the discussion. My goal wasn't to embarrass and/or color judgments in the dialog.

Students learned they were writing for an audience that did not necessarily share their tastes. The *Hoosier-Record's* readers were older. The students began to recognize, in short, that they were not the center of the universe. Their job was to produce story content for a paying audience that had expectations different than theirs.

Imagine a total stranger is looking over your shoulder as you write, was my mantra, and he or she is your sole audience. Keep it understandable. "What if this person doesn't speak English?" That was a response I once received from one of my quicker quipsters. "Play it by ear," was my stock answer.

I always made sure to toss in a feature-writing idea or two of my own in our mixes. Typically it would be one that was totally out of place for a rural, weekly newspaper. This meant film reviews, pro sports, rock stars, national politics, fashion, and anything "Kardashian" were out. Nothing op-ed, first person, or judgmental. Speculation? Conjecture? Only if it came directly from someone in the story.

Without direct access to subjects or narrative, almost always there was no credence unless attribution was noted. The *Hoosier-Record* was a weekly and not a daily. You could assume readers went elsewhere for the big, breaking stories.

"Is this what they mean by 'making facts matter,'" asked Tyvonia, always a quick study. "Seems kind of boring."

That's the challenge, I said. *Don't* make it boring. "And don't get lazy and think your first draft is all you need. A great mystery writer like Elmore Leonard said it best. If your writing sounds like writing, rewrite it."

Chapter 17

In Their Spare Time

Dwayne Johnson, chair of Harrison College's math department, likely is the school's most esteemed, honored professor. His PhD was earned at Iowa State University, where his seminal dissertation in applied statistics is considered by experts as pure genius. Dwayne also is a devoted beer can collector.

Yes, beer cans. He's amassed over a thousand cans---glass *and* metal, thank you---tucked away in a storage rental space. His pride and joy is an unopened 1937 Old St. Louis bottle valued at $8,000.

Mary Ann Robinson is the music department's piano instructor. She also doubles as the chapel organist for the school's annual holiday performance of Handel's Messiah and other special occasions. She spends summers as a Habitat for Humanity volunteer, having once worked with Jimmy Carter shingling a roof in 95-degree Alabama weather.

Bruce Marr, associate professor in classical languages with a specialty in Greek, is a confirmed birdwatcher. In addition to being recording secretary for the Southern Indiana Birdwatchers Association (SIBA), he is the perennial winner of the state's Big Bird event in which contestants have 24 hours to make sightings. Bruce's latest target is a Dark-eyed Junco, a not-so-rare species that somehow has eluded him.

Harrison students would not have to wander far from campus to find feature stories for the *Hoosier-Record*. The faculty was fertile ground. Tricky too. Some professors consider their pastimes strictly private—or, at the very least, material not to be handled by what they regarded as a laughable, local newspaper.

If the story wasn't written the way *THEY* wanted, and it was my policy not to show stories in advance (except to Newt, of course), it could lead to trouble. Not everyone felt that way, of course. Some faculty members appreciated my students' efforts. They understood the value in this exercise.

Enter: Ron Pfister, who teaches in the art department. His story was can't-miss.

By Daniel Newman
& Jennifer Day
Special to the Hoosier-Record

How did you spend your summer break? Working? Playing? Studying?

A mere week before classes started, Harrison College Art Professor Ron Pfister finished a project that took many months to finish. A devoted bicyclist, he completed a unique, solo ride across the U.S. on his Trek 1000 Road Bike.

"It was the fulfillment of a lifelong dream for me," he said. "I've biked the Erie Canal, Iowa's RAGBRAI ride, Bike Virginia, Katy Trail from St. Louis to Kansas City, and a bunch more, but they only made me want to try crossing the entire U.S. and not simply pieces of it."

The professor's trip connected the country's southern tier between San Diego at one end and Jacksonville, Florida, at the other. He clocked approximately 3,000 miles in close to 60 days *of pedaling. His ride also doubled as a fundraiser, raising a little over $6,700 in donations for several environmental-related charities.*

The adventure started last winter in an unusual fashion. He rode in separate increments, or segments, that ranged from three days to two weeks---but each segment was in an opposite direction!

"The first segment was west-to-east, *San Diego to Yuma in Arizona," said Professor Pfister. "Then my second installment was east-to-west, Jacksonville to Tallahassee, alternating in opposite directions each time."*

When there were openings on his calendar, the professor would fly with his bike to the point where he last finished a segment and continued the journey.

"I plotted it carefully," he said. "I calculated how far I could make it to the best, or any, accommodations. I rented cars to get to airports. I called ahead in many cases to make logistical arrangements.

"I met a lot of nice people. Biking is like one big family. When necessary, Lorna (his wife) would take me to my starting point or be waiting at a terminal spot in a car."

The finish line, where it can be said he met himself in opposite directions, was Bentonville, Arkansas. "This was about halfway," he said. "I'm pretty sure I'm the first biker to pedal across the country and complete my adventure in Arkansas, the middle."

The trek went about as well as expected. He weathered four flat tires, two broken chains, heavy downpours in Mississippi and Louisiana, a snake in his sleeping bag in Texas ("Not sure if it was a rattler. I didn't ask."), three spills that resulted in skinned knees and elbows, and a week's worth of 110-plus-degree days in Arizona.

Note 1: He wore a helmet whenever he was pedaling.

Note 2: He encountered minimal road rage.

Though his intention was to accumulate as many miles daily as possible on each increment, the professor couldn't resist a little sightseeing along the way---if it didn't require too much time or distance off his path. These diversions included the Grand Canyon in Arizona, site of the Manhattan atomic bomb project in Los Alamos in New Mexico, and the Pettus/Freedom Bridge in Selma, Ala.

"I could write a book about this trip, and maybe I will," said Professor Pfister. "I did some sketching along the way. I do know I was very glad to complete the trip."

He pedaled into Bentonville in mid-afternoon on a sweltering Tuesday in August. He rode past Wal-Mart's unassuming national headquarters on 8th Street and the spectacular Crystal Bridges Museum of American Art a few blocks from the courthouse square.

It was there on the town square's lawn, in a total surprise to Professor Pfister 25 or so friends---Harrison College colleagues, and former students---organized by Lorna, greeted him with cheers and blasts from horns.

Their numbers soon swelled with curious locals after the professor plunged through "The finish: Great job" banner stretched across the sidewalk. Then, just to make things official, he turned around and went through the finish line in the opposite direction.

"According to my calculations, I could meet myself somewhere in Arkansas and say I rode my bike across the country. I picked Bentonville.

Why?

"I always wanted to see that Crystal Bridges Museum of American Art that Wal-Mart built there. It's a real winner. Worth the effort, in my book. If I return, I'll drive there in a car."

Chapter 18

Raising Stakes

Princess Casino employees knew little about their employers. But paychecks didn't bounce and that always was a good start.

Most workers were aware the boat was owned by something named Bel-Tar, part of a Detroit-based, private capital group. The organization kept its financial dealings and holdings secretive---and then some---as allowed by the Internal Revenue Service (IRS) and all other alphabet-soup government agencies.

Some employees knew three other casinos anchored on the Kentucky side of the Ohio River were also part of Bel-Tar. Occasionally, employees got shuffled within the fleet system---The Queen, The Duchess, The Countess, and The Princess---and made it easy to pass on office gossip to co-workers.

Big Brother might be watching, of course. After all, it was a casino with money flying fast and furious. Someone was always looking over their shoulders, but there was no questioning everyone was part of one, big gaming operation with the Feds occasionally checking the books. Rumors were as plentiful as poker chips.

The employees---dealers, roulette wheel spinners, hosts, floor security, kitchen help, floor walkers, valet parkers, kitchen help, front line cashiers, and auditors---had become aware of a recent uptick in business. However, they had no idea about Bel-Tar plans to make that revenue grow even larger.

Certainly, that was the takeaway from an unscheduled and unexpected meeting in the Princess on an otherwise quiet weekday afternoon. That's when The Princess manager, Pete Stanley, was startled to walk into his office and see Sam Rozner, No. 2 in the overall casino boat chain-of-command, sitting in Pete's chair with his feet propped up on his desk.

Any anxiety was erased quickly when Sam, breaking into a big smile, stood up to shake Pete's hand. "Just happened to be in the neighborhood, Pete, and thought we"---nodding toward Rick, his security chief/driver standing near the door---"would drop in for a visit. I'm a little late getting around to this, but congratulations are in order."

"Err, thanks," said Stanley, with no idea why he was being congratulated.

Sam went on to explain the Princess's numbers, closely monitored by Bel-Tar bean counters, were far ahead of previous years in every category. Clearly, Pete's boat was on course to top the other three casinos in the group. This would be a first. The explanation seemed obvious.

"It's the sports book," said Sam. "Our guys went over and over the numbers. Broke it all down, then it became perfectly obvious. Now that the Princess can offer legal betting on all sports events---not just horse racing and card games, and the slots---you're headed for the moon.

"I mean who doesn't want to lay down money, *LEGALLY*, on Michigan and Ohio State in football? Or Notre Dame and Southern California? Or what about Indiana playing Kentucky in hoops? Especially with all those celebrity endorsers."

Thanks to federal legislation, placing bets on sports events now was legalized on a state-by-state basis. Indiana was one of those ratifying the new rules. Kentucky was not. This meant the three boats moored in Kentucky waters saw this new vein of betting revenue cross the bridge into Indiana and presumably to the nearest Indiana game room, the Princess.

In the Princess, everything from Major League Baseball and pro football to college athletics and cricket in England was fair game---and had been for six months. Furthermore, the margin was helped by a lower tax rate in Indiana and Harrison County where the boat was docked. The Princess was hiring!

On the other side of the river in Kentucky, where the state legislature had not ratified the new mandate, there was no idea if, and when, all-sports sports betting would become legal. The Queen, The Duchess, and The Countess were stuck in the mud. The horse racing lobby was powerful in the Bluegrass State and saw more liberalized wagering as a threat.

And ouch: the state and county on the Kentucky side took bigger tax bites from the three boats. As a result, those casinos were laying off employees.

"I wasn't exactly sure where we ranked with the other three boats," said Pete, "I was kind of hoping for this uptick. This is good to know. I'm a little surprised it's as high as you indicate. I think we can do even better."

And that was the point of Sam's visit.

"Glad to hear that. I'm here to help you do exactly that," he said. "Back in Detroit, we've been studying this closely and have a few---shall we say---marketing and bookkeeping ideas to put in play."

These would include increased advertising in local media, distribution of discount coupons, holiday-themed decorations and giveaways, sponsorships of outside events, concerts, and extensive online marketing.

"We need to build a much larger databank of customers and potential customers, whether they have been bettors or not," Sam added. "We've got to get our message out there even more now that things are turning. If it remains this good without much push, just think what we can do raising our profile with the general public, and not just bettors. That's what our marketing people tell us, anyway."

One source for adding names to the mailing list, insidious as it sounded to Pete, was planting "spies" in local Gamblers Anonymous chapters. "This person could simply observe others, see who might be a prospect to---you might say---return to the fold," pointed out Sam. "Then, we get them on a separate media list with special incentives."

On the construction side, Sam said a small hotel was in the long-range plans. Now, simply turning the parking lot into four or five levels instead of one also was on the drawing board. Creating a shuttle bus service from nearby Evansville and several other ports seemed logical. Maybe all the way from Louisville.

"For sure there'll be one or two ferry boats in Kentucky that'll cross the river, drop customers right at the Princess's doorstep," he added. "We see building a first-rate daycare center, something to keep kids occupied while Mom and Dad gamble. Maybe even a small theater for kid movies. They'll grow up to become bettors someday like Mommy and Daddy.

"Let's face it. The longer we can keep customers in the house, the more we'll get out of them. The odds favor it." This last reference made Sam laugh.

"Sounds ambitious," said Pete, with a forced smile. Deep down, he had reservations about casino gambling becoming, shall we say, a family affair. Targeting kids seemed kind of low.

Sam had several more items on his list, including personnel changes and a new accounting system. He also was setting up what he labeled Bel-Tar Internships, a "special" program in which part-time and summer jobs would be made available to college students at designated schools.

By now, Pete had tuned out his boss, and, in the end, merely nodded at more plans he cited.

He perked up with Sam's final declaration.

"Gambling is going to own college and pro sports. You can see it now. Pro football and college athletics have become as greedy as it gets. Now so-called amateur athletes will be getting paid. The gambling industry will be side-by-side picking up tabs. TV, too. Bel-Tar wants to be at the head of the line."

Pete felt he needed a shower when Sam was finished. This was not what he signed up for as boss of The Princess. After walking Sam and Rick to their car, he returned to his office and took no more calls or visitors the rest of the afternoon. Gambling, a family affair? Luring busted Gamblers Anonymous members back to the fold? Hiring impressionable college jocks for what purpose, God only knows.

Chapter 19

Library Overdue

Harrison's two worlds---the college campus and surrounding town---rarely converged on big issues. When they did, generally it was news .... hard news for local media outlets. The college's sporting events were the obvious meeting places. There always was a sprinkling of local athletes on the Harrison College Generals' teams to help serve as a draw. On the flip side, concerts and theater productions rarely drew townies.

Nevertheless, these intersections did not always get covered by the *Hoosier-Record* because of the work it entailed. They were handled in the paper via college news releases that sugar-coated everything. Newt was the only full-time editorial staffer. He also edited contributions from part-time staff, took pictures, wrote headlines, sold advertising, laid out and oversaw delivery of his paper.

Newt was further hamstrung by the fact his publication was a weekly, meaning some of the newsier stories were old news before readers got to his publication by the end of the week. Rarely did he post breaking news on his *Hoosier-Record* web site unless it involved death or bad weather.

For Newt, who had a good nose for stories, watching them slip from his grasp was ultra-frustrating. "Like watching a record-breaking trout slip off the hook," he liked to say.

With close supervision by me, there was plenty of room in this mix for stories by my stable of student authors. Mostly our mix consisted of soft, readable features. They were welcomed by Newt, otherwise we could be putting the newspaper and school at risk with "hot" stories. Too many chances for errors.

With a little digging there was good material for us in Harrison, and it was easy for me to get wind of it at Rotary luncheons. Newt also kept a list he hoped to tackle at future dates. Rarely did that date arrive.

Yes, if it wasn't on the police blotter and part of the public record, the chances were slim that anything juicy got reported. Newt was methodical about covering city council and school board meetings, but, yawn, rarely did those groups stray from their boring agendas.

"Occasionally there's a nutty, over-the-top parent at a school board meeting," he said. "Things always go off the tracks a bit at election time, too, especially if its presidential. Nobody really seems to pay much attention to local government offices."

No one could have predicted that Harrison, as a home to two libraries---the college's Grabbe Library and the town's Harrison Public Library---would become an issue. But here it was: What about merging them? Save a few dollars?

No one was quite sure how the idea got started. The notion was floated at least once a decade. Things quieted when the college opened its doors two years ago to Harrison residents, allowing them library cards with full access and privileges. Few availed themselves.

A merger of the two libraries did seem practical. But how would you go about it? The college's library is three up-to-date floors of books, periodicals, meeting rooms, mini museum, and rows and rows of computers. No expense gets spared to keep its technology up-to-date and purring.

The building, designed by a Chicago architect and erected in the mid-1950s, is on a hillside providing spectacular floor-to-ceiling views of a distant valley and the winding Tippecanoe River.

Featured as a backdrop in the school's official logo, the library structure is historically landmarked and occasionally a destination for tourists. The autumn colors are worthy of a Grant Wood painting.

Among distinguished, visiting lecturers within its walls have been poet Robert Frost, writer Carl Sandburg, activist Martin Luther King, and author Beverly Cleary.

It was not unusual for faculty and townspeople alike to be seen patronizing the snack bar as soon as the doors open on weekday mornings. That's when the baked goods, prepared and brought over from a nearby dormitory dining hall kitchen, are most plentiful and fresh. The scones were once featured on a PBS-TV cooking show.

Then there is Harrison's municipal library. The location is two blocks off the Harrison city square in one direction and two blocks from the college campus in the opposite direction. There's no mistaking its Carnegie Library legacy, with the squarish, fading and chipped red brick facade, cracked mortar patchwork, dull white trimmed windows and columns framing the front entrance.

Nameless now, most locals simply refer to it as "the Old Carnegie"---a product of the famed industrialist's financing of over 2,500 libraries beginning in the late 19th century. Old-timers can recall that for a few years in the 1950s it was named the Fosdick Library. Born in Harrison, Fredrick (Fred) Fosdick became one of Indiana's wealthiest natives with patents and production of recycled automobile tires. Among his non-profit causes---and tax dodges---was a generous annual donation to the Carnegie in the community where he was raised.

Then, when it was discovered that Fred also was a major financial supporter of efforts to resurrect Indiana's once active, racist Ku Klux Klan organization, his nameplate came down. Wisely, the decision was made a week after his annual, six-figure check arrived for the upcoming year.

The library was opened in 1910. A large picture of the dedication ceremony greets visitors above the checkout counter. The black-and-white photo shows a ribbon being cut by the first librarian, a handle-bar mustachioed J. Arthur Crosby. Behind him are Indiana Gov. Thomas Marshall and Harrison Mayor Myron G. Oglethorpe.

The photo of the Harrison Library dedication is an insightful, realistic glance into American history. In the background are vintage, dark-colored automobiles with starter cranks and skinny-spoked tires parked alongside stationary horses and buggies.

Almost every male in the crowd is dressed in a conservative, black suit, and white shirt with a tight and tall collar, vest, and bowler. About half of the males are leaning on canes.

The women present wore long and flowery Sunday-best dresses with who-knows-what underneath. They wore wide-brimmed and colorful hats festooned with colorful ribbons, and most carried an umbrella for shade.

Among the library's distinguished guests have been U.S. Vice-Presidents Dan Quayle and Mike Pence, and civil rights activist Vernon Jordan, an alum of upstate DePauw University.

It's not true that the current Harrison librarian, Miss Alva Stone, was somewhere in that picture (which would make her roughly 120 years old) ---though some modern-day patrons feel she'd fit.

As long as any living, breathing soul in Harrison County can recall, Miss Stone---she never married---was the chief librarian.

Her tenure touched three generations of readers. Only a handful of those library users ever saw her smile, generally at the expense of a patron's display of ignorance.

She treated the books as if they were her private property. "*50 Shades of Grey*" never had a chance in her library. Though there is no such thing as a banned book, she was known to not let readers check out books she deemed inappropriate for them.

Repeat: She wouldn't allow customers to check out books that were on display. It was called getting "Stone-walled."

New patrons got thoroughly interrogated, right down to having their educational background noted on his or her library card application. "This way, I will know what you should be reading," was her condescending explanation. Newcomers were at her mercy and, as a result, were known to time their checkouts when Alva was at lunch.

An overdue book? If it went past a week, Miss Stone personally called the delinquent reader and asked for a return. If it went much longer, she was known to go to the home of the "miscreant" and personally request an on-the-spot handover.

The "Old Carnegie" has three PCs for public use. Alva's assistant, Becky Barnes, handles any record-keeping or communications requiring modern technology. Alva prefers to use her pet, non-electric typewriter. She hunts and pecks the keys, then turns her content over to Becky for entry into what she liked to cynically refer to as "the technological stratosphere."

The bookcase that highlights best-sellers is almost a decade behind the New York Times' list. Nobody knows for sure how many books are available for readers. They'd be afraid to ask Alva.

Curiously there is no used public library book sale, but residents continually dump books and book-related artifacts at the doorstep. Nothing gets tossed after getting in Alva's hands. Deep in several basement rooms, stacks and stacks of unrecorded novels, expired library cards, bookmarks, posters, old newspapers, photo albums---some a century or more old---and other materials are piled behind Alva's lock and key.

Miss Stone *is* the public library, or WAS the Harrison Public Library until that day in September, when Becky found Alva in her office slumped---dead---over the typewriter. In a touch of irony, there was a "Shhh! You're in a library" sign on the desktop next to her typewriter.

Her passing left Harrison's City Council with a dilemma. In the last few decades ageless Alva's unchallenged, iron-fisted rule had kept the library woefully out-of-date and scared many readers away. Some swore they'd never return, jumping at the chance to use the college library when it "went public."

A major Carnegie overhaul was needed.

Over the years she asked for little from her board in the way of upgrades and budget increases, preferring not to draw attention or having strings attached to filling her request. It was a big deal when Alva finally broke down and took out subscriptions three years ago to the *Wall Street Journal* and *New York Times.*

In addition to basic repairs and general patchwork mending of the building, adding air conditioning, overhaul of content (periodicals, videos, CDs) and modern technology were sorely needed.

Programming? Start with this: Harrison may have had the only library in Indiana without a book club. Its children's section consisted of three shelves and a mere three Dr. Seuss works.

To bring things up to speed with Alva no longer blocking the way, an overhaul would be expensive. For starters, a search for a new head librarian would be necessary. Becky Barnes had no interest. From her viewpoint, an entire reload would be needed above and beyond the typical, modern librarian challenges.

Since the college library kept an open door for townspeople as well as students, a steady stream of locals had begun using it---with the snack bar's baked goods for sure an added, popular attraction.

President Casey was willing to have the college make room for the city facility to be merged with the Grabbe. Undoubtedly there would be volume overlap, which meant the inventory wouldn't be as great as some might think. Maybe find a way for the Carnegie to occupy a full floor. The public facility could then be razed to become a new municipal building or remodeled for re-purposing. The city definitely could use the space.

The idea of the college taking on the public library as a partner was intriguing when the concept first made its way to President Casey. To be honest, he---and just about everyone else in Harrison---never thought Alva Stone would die.

Nothing was official and there was much on his plate early in the school year, but there was no question that a merger was a perfect fit for his Town & Gown push.

Chapter 20

Digging In

The official gatherings of the ad hoc library merger committee tended to be fast, efficient, and indecisive. The group's makeup: City, or non-college connected, would get two spots with the college also getting two seats, and Mayor Lorna Tobin being the designated tie-breaker as the fifth member.

Richard Webber, or *Doctor* Richard Webber as he preferred, quickly seized the group's unofficial leadership role ...... just as he aggressively lobbied President Casey for one of the college's two committee spots.

"I've spent more time in libraries than anyone living," he said at the initial meeting. It was an attempt to be humorous but it sounded a lot more hubristic than funny. Smiles were forced.

With no telling what lay in store for them, no committee member---besides Webber---expressed interest in leading the effort. "He wants it, he can have it," was the unspoken feeling among the others.

No doubt Webber had degrees from prestigious schools, including a PhD from the University of Wisconsin-Madison, but it was obvious to anyone in his presence he never took a course in humility. His Mr. Chips wardrobe, deep in ties, wrinkle-free button-downed shirts, occasional vests, and tweed jackets---some with elbow patches---spelled academic arrogance. All that was missing was a pipe. He didn't smoke.

The committee, though advisory, had the backing of both the Harrison City Council and college trustees. Their conclusions and recommendations would be taken seriously. In addition to Webber, the members were the college's Dean of Student Affairs, Dr. Julie Frank; Barney DeWitt, a local businessman whose wife belonged to two book clubs; and Anne Stegora, a realtor and next-door neighbor of Mayor Tobin.

I made sure to have at least a student or two in attendance. Obviously, this was a developing story that would benefit from depth and context. Newt took in a few sessions, but soon he was confident enough to lean on my students' input.

Barney was president of the Harrison Chamber of Commerce and a Rotarian. His ongoing Harrison Library memory was a very public scolding he once received from Alva for an overdue book. He was 36 years old at the time. Anne was a realtor, Rotarian and the mayor's next-door neighbor. She was big on Danielle Steele novels.

Julie Frank? She was a relative newcomer to Harrison College, having been hired two years earlier as Dean of Student Affairs. She was an avid reader, especially creative nonfiction, and full of innovative programming ideas she wanted to offer and get implemented.

Julie was not a Rotarian. The committee was her first official foray into the Harrison public community, and President Casey was watching her response closely. Unknown to any of the college's hierarchy, he had her pegged as the future replacement for the school's imperious Dean Brunk.

Tours were the first order of the committee's business. Barney DeWitt and Anne Stegora had never set foot in the campus's Grabbe Library. Well, the coffee shop for fresh baked goods, yes. The book stacks, no.

One thing became perfectly clear to everyone: A very expensive overhaul and installation of technology "tekkie do dads" (Barney's words) would be in the offing for the "Old Carnegie" if it was to remain a library.

The college reps were split on the public library: Webber said there had been occasions when he searched for periodicals---namely the *New York Times* and *The Week* magazine---in the Carnegie. Frank never had been in the municipal facility.

Everyone was concerned that a merger would create excess noise and overcrowding in either of the two facilities. "There's some serious research that takes place in the Grabbe," noted Webber. "Some accommodation needs to be in order for those people to have access to what we expect from any library---a quiet place to work."

In the end, the committee was right back where it started---but leaning toward a merger with the Grabbe as the logical landing spot for a unified library. The Carnegie easily could be re-purposed by the city for other uses---city council chambers, municipal offices, whatever.

The merger would mean a complete overhaul of duplicate offerings. For instance, both libraries had large best-seller sections. Or, as Anne Stegora put it: "No matter what we decide, we have to comb through everything to look for overlap. I mean how many John Grisham's do you need? We could end up having the state's largest used book sale."

Something they all agreed upon: A study commissioned by the committee and done by a University of Illinois library consultant was basically worthless, considering it did not offer much more than the committee itself observed after their tours.

Everyone agreed: "That was $5,000 down the drain as far as I'm concerned," said Webber. "A waste of money. Not a good start for us." He was particularly concerned that no insights about Alva's locked, basement storage rooms were forthcoming.

"I'll find the key and inspect them for us. There's got to be something in there worthwhile."

Chapter 21

Report Card

It was obvious Becky Barnes was not the person to succeed Alva Stone as chief librarian whether the library landed on campus or remained in the present location. She was too timid, or so it seemed.

Not that she wanted the job. Becky had been Alva's chief--- and lone full-time--- assistant for close to 15 years, but never appeared to harbor ambitions to advance beyond that role. She was happy to have a respectable position that, while not making her rich, carried a certain degree of prestige and security for someone without a college degree.

Any ambitious moves up a career ladder might require a move to another town. Becky was born and raised in Harrison. To her this was the center of the universe---not something to escape.

Undoubtedly there would be a role for her somewhere in the yet-to-be-determined order, but she had been perfectly content to be Alva's diligent assistant all those years rubber stamping anything tossed her way. Ironically, that is exactly what could make her valuable to the committee.

"Whew! Ain't much that woman don't know about the library and books," said Barney DeWitt, after the committee's debriefing of Becky. "If you gotta dig for something, she'll find the answers. No matter which way we go, down the road she could be valuable."

"Yes, well, that's probably so," jumped in committee chair Webber. "It certainly was obvious to me she would never work in an executive role. No degree. Not even a BA. Still, I do agree that she could be useful."

There was a slight pause here.

Barney started to respond, then caught himself, and clammed up. The mayor, Lorna Tobin, noting a potential rift developing within the group, quickly changed the subject. "So where do we go from here?" asked Tobin.

Each committee member had been asked to take individual tours of the Harrison Public Library and the Grabbe Library. There had been dozens of questions for a squirming Becky, who, as everyone understood, had been strictly under Alva's thumb.

Their observations after touring the Harrison Public Library were almost unanimous. Here were a few in no special order:

"The place needs a new roof."

"I could see paint peeling on the ceilings."

"Do we have any good stone masons in Harrison? That brick stairway in front has some mighty big chips and nicks."

"Only three computers for public use?"

"No *Chicago Tribune* in the periodical section?"

"The men's room was closed for repairs. I came back three days later, and it was still closed. Unacceptable. What does a man do? Go outside and pee behind a bush?"

"Closed all day Sunday? Couldn't it be open for a few hours in the afternoon?"

"Handicap accessibility was through a rear door. That doesn't seem right."

If there was one thing that piqued everyone's curiosity about the city library, it was this: What's in the locked storage rooms? No one gained access on his or her visit.

"I'd like to know myself," said Becky. "I lost my key a long time ago. Miss Stone always promised to have another one made for me but never did. It was on her to-do list. She had one key for herself, but she kept it hidden away.

"I do know the space is full of books, or at least was full of them before I lost my key. It's where we'd stick all the stuff that people dropped off. Old books, mostly, but also posters, old newspapers, magazines.

"Miss Stone always said that someday we'd clear it out and have a rummage sale. Never did."

Before anything could happen, the decision would have to be made whether (1) the libraries consolidated. Yes or no?

If they did, that would mean (2) the current Harrison public facility would be taken over by the city for another use, and (3) its viable contents moved to new space on the campus in the Grabbe.

From the very start, President Casey made it known the Grabbe, whatever the decision, was not moving. It was inconceivable, he said, that the Old Carnegie could ever accommodate the school's needs---let alone be eight blocks from classrooms.

Mayor Tobin, keeping the committee on point, said, "We really couldn't start a search for Alva's replacement until we know where the city library will be located. Our immediate business is to make a recommendation to the city council. In the end, it's their call."

Chapter 22

Status Report 1

"Kansas State! You're going to Kansas State!!"

"Whoa, cowboy," countered Mary. "I haven't said yes, and it's too early for anything. I did have a good conversation with the school. By Zoom. Someone from its College of Liberal Arts and someone from the ag school. I've got another call with someone in the academic dean's office.

"I don't know if there's an offer in all of this. I'm not committing to anything 'til I visit the campus. It's in Manhattan."

My reply, "Yeah, the wrong one. Kansas is in the middle of nowhere."

The silence and stare that followed told me I'd better mellow out at this point. After all, Mary is a native of Kansas. Also, we both knew the day would come that one, or both of us, would have to move to take another college job. We'd never had a real disagreement before. This was new turf. Tread softly, big guy.

The 10,000-pound gorilla in the room was: Mary was a helluva lot more marketable than me. We didn't say it, but it was true. She, with her PhD, knew how to play the "academic game." All I was good at was putting out fires for President Casey. God forbid he should leave.

It was not unusual a college would be so eager want to hire someone that a job was created for his or her spouse. I could name such package deals on our own Harrison campus. But Mary and I were not married. And, in the few conversations we'd had about one of us getting a tempting offer, we pretty much ignored the subject.

That was then. This was now---or was it?

The Kansas State offer was tempting. Mary's work on im-migration---legal or otherwise---and its impact on farming and connected food industries in the Upper Midwest was both timely and ground-breaking. Towns, on the brink of disappear-ing, were becoming revitalized mostly by Spanish-speaking migrants.

She was told the university was prepared to add relevant courses, and create a related, to-be-named minor tailored for both the sociology department and agricultural school. She would be given course relief and a $100,000-plus salary to get the program up and running.

Mary also would have full-time staff assistants as well as teaching contributions from other departments. "I was told there'd be a good chance this could be moved up from a minor to a major," she added. "But that would be some time off."

"And what about Arizona State, your alma mater? Weren't there opportunities there? What's the skinny there? Have you heard anything from them?"

"Nothing, really---yet," said Mary. "The positions aren't of-ficially open at this point. There are several that would be perfect, but everything's conjecture now. Applications from people like me don't mean much until someone gets in a panic. They go in the 'to be opened late' file. There have to be resignations before openings and searches. Friends tell me one rumor has ASU eliminating, instead of filling, some positions.

"Teaching at Kansas State would be a hoot, considering I'm from Kansas, and my brothers and Dad live there. We'll have to wait and see."

No comment on her usage of "we." ASU was a much larger university, three times the size of KSU. Its creative writing school has a great reputation. Maybe there'd be something for me.

Little could we know then another career decision *was* just around the corner for me, too.

Chapter 23

Status Report 2

"Chairman! Of the English Department? No shit! Really?"

That was Mary's not totally unexpected, unfiltered, and immediate reaction to my subsequent job news.

"Really, gal, was it that shocking?"

Within an hour of leaving President Casey's office---and a day after my confab with Mary at Whitey's about her future, I still was catching my breath. My first call with news the president wanted me to be the English chair was to Mary.

In my meeting with President Casey it worked like this: "John's in bad shape," said the president, referring to Dr. Schackelford. "That cough he developed? Surely, you've noticed it like everyone else. I can't get into the particulars of the disease, but, in short, he's developed a form of throat cancer. He's not a smoker anymore, either. He put down his pipe long before I arrived. A real shame."

The president said that Professor Schackelford thought he could get through the entire school year as English Department chair. Instead, upon his doctor's advice and encouragement from his wife, Hazel, he was retiring at the end of the first semester.

"Nearly 40 years here," added President Casey. "It's a sad ending. I told him there'd always be a place for him. He was grateful to hear this, but said he'd been considering retirement anyway. Wanted to spend more time with his gardens. He's quite a gardener, you know. Won some prizes, too. I guess his Petunias are unmatched."

And?

"If we'd known this at the start of the Fall term, we would have launched a search for a permanent replacement by now," he added. "Maybe we would've hired someone from inside, or maybe go outside for the new department chair. But a full-scale search---a year long—is called for at this level. We're going to take our time."

Casey explained that he wanted me to be the English Department chair "pro tem" while the search was organized and conducted.

"We'll stumble through the second semester this year with the job essentially vacant, but with you---as interim---handling basic decisions. You'd be the acting English Department chair through next year while the search process continued. Of course, we'd lighten your teaching load to one course, just like John was doing."

Then, there was this gem that brought music to my ears: "If everything went well, you'd be a strong candidate for the job on a permanent basis."

Now there were a million questions going through my head. First and foremost: Will there be objections to me becoming the interim chairman? Surely Dean Brunk objects. He's a stickler for protocol and he's in charge of academics at Harrison. There have to be other more qualified Harrison faculty. I don't have a PhD. I don't have tenure. Yikes! I'd love to see the reaction of Webber, a stickler for academic protocol, to my news.

Casey explained that the move was perfectly within *his* province. This was an administrative decision, and not academic, he explained. He was---in effect---Harrison College's chief administrator, according to the bylaws, and answered only to the board of trustees. Though he had not run it by them, there was no precedent for the board overriding his choices for department chairs.

"I can't imagine Dean Brunk would approve of this," was my response. "Surely he'll raise the roof. He's such a purist. In his mind my credentials are too slim just to teach, let alone be a department chairman."

"He'll get over it," countered the president. "Besides, in addition to me, the only other person I've consulted on this is a big supporter of this move. This person likes you a lot for the position. In fact, it was his suggestion."

Who?

"Professor Schackelford himself, the outgoing chair. He's a big fan of your work. He thinks you'd be great in this role. The school could use---and these are his words---'a little shot of adrenalin.'

"And, I totally agree," said the president.

Chapter 24

Moving On Up

The president gave me a day to consider accepting the new position. This, of course, called for a quick rally of minds that night with Mary at our seat of all wisdom---Whitey's tavern.

Should I accept---a non-move that could have a direct bearing on her shifting employment landscape? Or should I decline and remain flexible to follow her at either Kansas State or Arizona State? If there were no jobs for me teaching at either place, I could always return to bartending.

To Mary I said: "I gotta take this opportunity at Harrison. How many times do I get a chance to move up in higher ed? The president made it sound almost like a lock the chairmanship would be mine if I wanted it. Just don't commit any felonies. He said I could even teach my writing course. The other department chairs teach a bit, too. You get secretarial support with the job.

"The amazing thing—at least to me---is this: Schackelford is my patron in all of this. I thought he was strictly old school... a Dean Brunk *yes-man* and all that. Guess he liked it that my classes were full. That, and my grip on technology."

This was when Whitey, spotting us huddled in a far booth, wandered over to impart his two cents and news of the day.

Little did he know what was in store for him with this innocent opening: "So what brings you two here in the middle of the week? You look a little stressed."

We unloaded. After all, if you can't trust your local bartender, who can you trust? We laid it all out for him, finally coming up for air with a promise that he'd keep things confidential for now.

"You got to take the Harrison offer, Flip," was his first response, "and I don't say that cuz' I don't want to lose a customer. Mary? You're trickier. Can you be sure Kansas State will come through with its plans? That's why you're going there. Get it in writing. Sounds like you'd have a lot of administrative work in front of you. Make sure you get help. Do you want that? Arizona State's already got things in place."

Well, there are other considerations besides the classroom.

"Yeah, yeah, I get it," he said. "You'd be separated. Damn, you teachers get enough time off; that shouldn't be a problem. Summers, holidays, long weekends. Probably a helluva lot easier to fly to Phoenix than drive to Manhattan...in nowhere Kansas. Especially in the winter."

Chapter 25

Underground Railroad Story by Students

As my students stretched for stories to get published in the *Hoosier-Record*, they learned a lot of local history. At the same time, it started to become obvious Harrison College was not quite the dark side of the moon with its rural, sparsely populated setting.

Some significant people lived or passed through the county, community, and college. There's plenty of evidence a youthful Abraham Lincoln undoubtedly---and repeatedly---was a Harrison visitor. The school's own namesake, Gen. William Henry Harrison, who became the ninth president of the United States, regularly led military maneuvers in this region of Indiana in the early 1800s.

Famous speakers made appearances here. A survivor of Custer's Last Stand was buried here. One of a handful of U.S. women to serve under combat conditions in the Vietnam War is a resident. Andrew Carnegie built a library here.

Maybe at the top of the list was this: Harrison had been a crossroads of Civil War friction. With the Ohio River boundary of the Mason-Dixon line only a few miles away, both abolitionist and Ku Klux Klan sentiments were alive and well and hotly disputed before and during---and sometimes after---the war between the states.

As far as I was concerned, this meant plenty of stories to be discovered and written.

Here was a gem for a feature story extracted---again---from a guest speaker at a Rotary luncheon. Within seconds after Dr. Dixon DeJarnett, an American history expert at Indiana University, concluded his remarks and slides that day covering the underground railroad, Newt and I agreed his presentation could be turned into great reading in his paper.

The result:

By Selma Forbes and Susan Smith
Special to the Hoosier-Record

The City of Harrison, seat of Harrison County, is a short drive to two separate interstate highways, 69 & 64. These major roadways give motorists the option of heading north to Indianapolis, south to Evansville, east to Louisville, or points west in Illinois.

Unknown to most area residents today is this: A major, northbound-only thoroughfare once cut straight through Harrison County. Few knew anything about this route, which was exactly the way users wanted it. This one-way artery led to freedom.

Popularly known as the Underground Railroad, it was part of a national network of clandestine routes and rest stops used by runaway slaves, their families, and guides---mostly on foot--- before and during the Civil War.

The travelers' goals were to escape mostly inhumane, but locally legal, bondage in southern states, which later seceded from the Union to become the Confederate States of America.

*The passageways were primarily traveled at night, typically us-
ing tunnels, little-utilized roads, forest trails, and farm fields in
all kinds of weather.*

*This important segment of American history left in its wake
many tales of courage that became popular material for books,
films, and TV. Legendary civil rights figures such as Harriett
Tubman and Fredrick Douglass "traveled" the railroad. Most re-
cently, writer Colson Whitehead's "The Underground Railroad"
book was both a Pulitzer Prize and National Book Award winner.
The TV series "Roots" also was a barrier breaker.*

*Opening their doors to provide rest, nourishment and tempo-
rary shelter from bounty hunters for the beleaguered travelers
were abolitionists such as legendary detective Allan Pinkerton,
Pennsylvania legislator Thaddeus Stevens, writers Harriett Beecher Stowe and Henry David Thoreau. Over decades of secret
use leading to the Civil War, it is estimated several hundred
thousand slaves gained freedom traveling the railroad.*

*One of the many routes on its spider-like, national map
passed through Harrison County.*

*One still-standing building in the city of Harrison has been
officially confirmed by historians as an underground railroad
safehouse. Shuttered and in serious disrepair, this is what is
locally known as "the old McPherson mansion" on the south
edge of town on Jackson Street.*

*At least two more structures in the county are rumored---
though not officially confirmed---as safehouses. "Locating and
certifying Underground Railroad stops is an ongoing project for
us," said Warren Barr, an archivist with the Indiana Historical
Society.*

*"For obvious reasons, there is no official paperwork to iden-
tify them, and this is exactly what makes Civil War history so
exciting. There are many discoveries still to be made."*

*Indiana was a free state and part of the Union in the Civil
War, but the entire southern* border adjacent to *Kentucky, a*

slave state and, though officially neutral at the start of the Civil War, a hotbed for Confederate sympathy. Separating these two states' entire, shared border was nearly a 300-mile stretch of the Ohio River, part of the Mason-Dixon line.

It took little effort for partisans on either side to cross the stream to conduct nefarious, disruptive deeds to either aid or hinder slave traffic. There were laws and local statutes---as slaves were considered property---that made it legal for run-aways to be hunted down and retrieved by bounty hunters and KKK members in Indiana.

The more zealous anti-slavery folk---abolitionists---on the Indiana side developed a counter: a network of welcoming hiding places---mostly large homes and barns---that created a path-way to Canada, and other safe northward locations, for African Americans fleeing southern bondage.

"It's difficult to imagine the hardships and downright fear slaves had to work through to travel this perilous journey," added Barr. "In most cases, these were families with children traveling on foot and trying to be invisible. Hundreds and hun-dreds of miles."

The goals tended to be two-fold: Make it to Canada, where slavery was banned, or a large U.S. city like Chicago or Detroit, where Blacks could assimilate into the general population with further help from relatives, family friends or an extension of aid from abolitionist guides.

"Most of what took place in this particular slaveholding movement went undocumented for obvious reasons," said Barr. "Mostly historians have to rely on diaries and newspapers that got passed down through generations for data. Meticulous records were kept, however, of transactions surrounding the buying and selling of slaves in states where it was legal to own them."

He added: Escapes to freedom have taken place in the U.S. since its earliest years. George Washington had 17 slaves bolt to *freedom in the years he was busy with the Revolutionary War. They were aided, Washington contended, by abolitionist-minded Quakers. Some of the most iconic figures in early American history, such as Thomas Jefferson, Benjamin Franklin, U.S. Grant, Andrew Jackson, Patrick Henry, and our own William Harrison, were slaveholders.*

It was a Quaker, Levi Coffin, who witnessed one of the Underground Railroad's most dramatic Ohio River crossings to freedom in this region. His account of the scene supposedly was the grist for Harriett Beecher Stowe's "Uncle Tom's Cabin" tale of Eliza Harris and her infant baby.

After escaping her slaveholder in northern Kentucky on a cold, winter night, she walked with her child to the Ohio River with the intention of crossing to freedom. Her motivation? She had learned that she was to be sold by her master and separated from her only surviving child. She already had buried two earlier infants.

Eliza made it across but not before heroically jumping and skipping on ice floes and, at times, sinking to her waist in water while holding her baby above her head. A historical marker on the river's shore marks the location of her desperate feat.

Eliza was joined by other fugitives when she reached the Indiana shore. Also waiting, was Coffin , who recorded this dash in his memoirs. He was an avowed abolitionist (common with Quakers) credited with aiding over 3,000 slaves gain freedom.

"Harrison, with its location, was an early stop on one of the routes northward," said Barr. "Pretty amazing feat to coordinate the rest stops. The McPherson's and their barns---sleeping in the hay lofts, sometimes with animals, that sort of thing---were welcoming.

"Sometimes, from what information we've obtained from the family descendants, as many as a dozen slaves populated this McPherson stop at one time. Of course, the goal was to keep the

human 'chain' moving deeper into the Union states and freedom. They walked at night and kept out of sight in daylight.

"The overriding strategy was to have runaways placed where
they could best escape if trouble materialized. They tended to be
better off in detached structures, away from where they could
be more easily trapped."

There is no real estimate of how many slaves made their way
on the Harrison route. There could've been additional rest stops
in the county, given the proximity to the Ohio River---and the
Mason-Dixon line. This made it very convenient.

The property has been sold and re-sold early in the 1900s.
Records show that the McPherson son who expected to inherit
the farm was killed in World War I trenches. Within a year, there
were new owners. The last owner failed to make a go of it as a
farmer and amid failing payments, the bank assumed ownership.

And the McPherson property's fate? It's been unoccupied for
more than a decade. The Harrison First National Bank holds
its title, and there have been at least two unsuccessful bidders.
Stumbling block? The amount of work needed to make it livable.
Spiders and rodents rule.

There is a large basement that could've accommodated run-
aways, but pictures in family albums show they are not the
original structures standing before the Civil War. Furthermore,
there is a quiet move to have the house and its 3,000-square
feet historically landmarked---hindering any major overhauls of
at least the structure's exterior.

Chapter 26

Breaking Through

Two weeks into individual inspections of the libraries' facilities, the committee members met as a group---and hit a wall. Well, not exactly a wall. It was the locked door to Alva Stone's municipal library storage room. An exhaustive search couldn't produce a key, and suspense was growing over what would be found. Theories ranged from rare books to dead bodies. Mice, for sure.

Becky Barnes was just as curious too. She had come up empty-handed in her search for the room's key. She was on hand for the 'unveiling.'

"Wouldn't miss it for the world," she told those gathered for the unveiling. After years of observing her autocratic boss toss all sorts of donated books and paper-filled packets into the room, her curiosity definitely was in overdrive.

For the long-awaited disclosure, the committee---Doctor Webber, Barney DeWitt, Anne Stegora, Julie Frank---gathered at the door to witness what everyone agreed would have to be a forced entry. They were joined by Harrison Mayor Lorna Tobin "Hey, I'm curious too."

Also on hand were two students from my writing class, Craig Marshall and Karen Garner, who had done a superb job on previous writing and reporting projects. At this point we weren't exactly sure what we would do with this as a story but knew something would be done. When informed of what was developing with the committee, it seemed a good idea to Newt to have someone on hand for a *Hoosier-Record* article.

In effect, this could be an important news story beyond the local paper as opposed to the mostly soft---but well-written--- feature articles my students churned out for his publication. If so, it could draw attention from state and regional news media outlets and, in turn, be good publicity for the college--- especially if something valuable was discovered. Collectibles were big in southern Indiana.

Everything came down to what Alva felt was worth saving and what should get tossed. Over the years there was a never-ending stream of materials dropped off in the library's drive-thru "donor barrel" on a loading dock behind the library.

The library's long-time janitor, Carlos Garcia, with tools in hand, was there to do door-crashing honors. "Miss Alva, she always tell me never, never bother to clean in here, so I never been inside," he told us as he began unscrewing door hinges and locks. "One night I come here, she was closing this door and turning off lights. It was too dark to see anything. Never I get closer to be inside in 12 years I work library."

Our best estimate, after looking at original blueprints for other Carnegie-designed libraries, pegged the space at approx-imately 30 x 40 feet (possibly larger) with a 12 x 15-foot ceiling. It was nestled into one back corner below the library's reference room.

Adding to the mystery, there were no windows and the pos-sibility of two floors---or at least of a functional, sub-basement level---for added stockpiling. The only entrance was now in Carlos's hands. Thus, there was no precise idea of the room's capacity for books or whatever else Alva deemed salvageable.

"Sometimes I saw Miss Stone carry an armload of material from the room," added Becky, "but I do not know what she did with it. Many times, she also took loads to the incinerator to burn. I was always thinking that those loads were damaged or useless materials. There were some good books she tossed out, too, but I never said anything."

The inside of the room after removing the door?

At first glance for the committee, it met expectations---dark, dusty, loaded with books and cardboard boxes filled with papers and pictures. And just to add a touch of color, the mice could be heard scurrying behind the piles.

Obviously, there was work ahead of the committee. Lots of it, but, being so fixated on gaining entry, no one knew exactly what to do next. Was there a goal? What were they looking for exactly?

"If nothing else," said Mayor Tobin, "we simply might add books to our current collections---no matter what the final library plan is. Right now this is the official property of the City of Harrison."

"Or the college," quickly countered Dr. Webber. "That is, if the Carnegie becomes merged and moved to the Grabbe, I assume the materials going to the school would be part of the transaction."

That would remain to be determined. For now, everyone simply figured there had to be some interesting reads in the piles before them. Other interesting stuff too. The county historical society might be interested, offered Mayor Tobin. Heck, maybe even the Indiana State Historical Society.

No record of the materials could be found, meaning everyone---the students jumped in as well---would start organizing in our best, impromptu Dewey Decimal System manner. There had to be several thousand books.

"We've got to get a more precise system before we do anything," said Dr. Webber. "Why don't two of us go through the non-book material.... Posters, old newspapers, anything that's been tossed and isn't a book, etc. That sort of stuff and look for something that might be historical. Then the rest of us go through books---separating them into nonfiction and fiction.

"Becky, as a trained librarian, can be a sort of an ombudsman, or trouble shooter. She can answer questions as we progress. Come to me, too. She and I probably are the best qualified to make filing judgments."

No one had been quite prepared for the task at hand. It was decided to give it a good 90 minutes, quit for the day, and return the following Saturday afternoon to finish the job. Hopefully. That's when a final decision would be made on what was salvageable. Becky, with her knowledge of what the library already possessed, promised to be on hand to expedite matters.

As they assessed their labors before departing, Barney De-Witt summed the experience up best: "I feel like we've been in a literature class. I learned a lot about books and authors."

Even Dr. Webber laughed.

Chapter 27

Here's David

On Saturday, committee members reassembled and went straight to work. The mayor didn't make this session. Pressing business, she said, and that was OK. Things were going smoothly.

It became increasingly obvious Alva stacked shelves and filled boxes in the locked room with no filing order in mind. Materials were loosely divided into topics such as biographies, gardening, cooking, best-selling fiction, history, prolific authors like James Patterson and John Grisham, wars, religion, politics (local and national), business, self-help, religion, sports, and biographies.

There were also stacks of newspapers, magazines, family albums, leaflets and posters in no special arrangement. Some newspapers were exceptionally old. They were handled with care to prevent crumbling.

At one point, it was a great surprise to learn Harrison had three newspapers---*Hoosier-Record*, *The Republican*, and *Freeman-Journal*. This was not unusual for the times before radio, television, the Great Depression and, of course, technology blew print media out of the water.

The town, though not much larger than its current population of approximately 12,000, was a hub of sorts in the late 1800s. There were regular Kentucky & Indiana Railway passenger train stops in a now-leveled station and 30-minute shuttle service---horse-drawn carriages in the early years---to a busy port on the Ohio River.

Apparently, two papers died during the depression. Two were weeklies, but the *Republican* published twice per week. While the *Freeman-Journal* and *Hoosier-Record* played their stories straight and soft, the *Republican* was a real history lesson for the times. Its stories were full of political nuances, and it was the party of progressive reform.

Several noteworthy, political campaign posters and fliers Alva had tacked to the wall. Dr. Webber perked up at spotting one handbill, which he estimated might have value as a collectible.

Collectibles? That was something that had not been seriously considered in our discussions. There was a leaflet boosting Abraham Lincoln's candidacy for president. It could have been one of those that flooded Chicago's old Wigwam Coliseum.

The story goes, according to the professor, that the Chicago Tribune publisher, Joseph Medill, a big fan of Lincoln's, had thousands of these printed to let fly from coliseum spectators when his nomination became official at the 1860 convention. It was probably worth something, he added.

It was hard to tell how the leaflet got to Harrison but the best guess was a delegate from Indiana brought it back, then it got passed down through descendants. Harrison attics appeared to be bottomless pits of stored items.

"Hey, look at this!" cried out Anne Stegora, a half-hour into sorting. "It's David Letterman!"

While it was well known that the former late night television host on TV was from Indiana, it was pretty obvious the person who dumped a "Letterman photo album" in the drive-thru donor barrel was a big fan.

The album included some weird stuff. For starters, there was a program from Letterman's graduation ceremony from Broad Ripple High School in Indianapolis. There were a few formal snapshots from his days at Ball State University. There also were pictures of his wives, articles cut from entertainment magazines, and an 8 x 10 photo of him in an embrace with Tonight Show host Johnny Carson.

"If he or she was so dedicated to Letterman, you have to wonder what made the fan give this away; spooky," said Anne.

"Maybe a stalker," said Barney, a comment met by momentary, frozen silence. "Sorry, bad comment."

The Letterman material was in a large box and shelves filled with what appeared to be reserved for "Hoosiers who made good" content---books about or by natives, magazine cover stories, prominently displayed newspaper articles, answers to fan letters, family photos, and posters.

Besides Letterman, a sampling included U.S. presidents William and Benjamin Harrison, U.S. vice-presidents Dan Quayle and Mike Pence, actresses Ann Baxter and Shelley Long, war correspondent Ernie Pyle, astronaut Gus Grissom, composer Cole Porter, singer Michael Jackson, writers Kurt Vonnegut, Theodore Dreiser and Booth Tarkington, poet James Whitcomb Riley, musician Hoby Carmichael, comedian Herb Shriner, the original Colonel Sanders, actor James Dean, aviation pioneer Wilbur Wright and, of course, Abraham Lincoln.

"We got us a real '*Antique Road Show*' here," said Barney. "Wonder if anything is worth anything."

Though no one was qualified to know for sure, it began to look as if some of Alva's secret stash could have value with collectors. Were there valuable first-edition books in the mix? Could some of the room's content have eBay value? It was beginning to look as if the committee's labors could turn into a fundraiser.

But who would benefit? Where does the money go? This sparked lively dialogue.

If there was a merger with the college's Grabbe Library, would proceeds be transferred to the school? If it remained in its present Andrew Carnegie facility as a municipal operation, there would be no question the benefits would be used to cover needed upgrades.

This could turn out to be one for lawyers.

"Let's not sweat it," said Barney. "It's probably not a big deal. I can't imagine this stuff would bring much. Maybe we could have a book sale and sell it by the pound."

Everyone laughed, but not Dr. Webber.

The unexpected variety of old materials being uncovered in Alva Stone's secret room had him thinking. There just might be valuable collectibles in the mix. He should know. After all, he was an American history professor with a PhD.

"What's this?" asked Barney, who held up a book titled "*The Life of Washington*" by Mason L. Weems. "I guess it goes with the biographies, or maybe history. I don't know. I've already run into a bunch of Washington stuff. What does everyone think?"

"Toss it," said Anne Stegora, holding a hand up with a thumb pointing downward. "That's what I've been doing when I see too much of one thing. Or let's leave it up to the professor."

It was late in the sorting session. The room was quite dusty. The committee members were getting tired; a bit giddy, too. Books were easy enough to handle, but they were becoming overwhelmed by the plethora of decisions to be made on the variety of items dropped all these years---decades---in the donor barrel.

"Oh, let's keep it," he said.

Chapter 28

The Plots Thicken

I had been given a day by President Casey to accept the offer to become interim chairman of the English Department. No need. My mind was made up by the time I left his office and walked several hundred yards to my office.

I'd be nuts to turn down this opportunity.

In addition to a nice pay raise, my teaching load would be lightened to one course per semester because of the extra administrative duties---and to be sure, I would make it my writing class that I keep up and running. Goodbye Chaucer, Keats, and Melville. Hello Truman Capote, J.K. Rawling, and J.D. Salinger.

Not bad for someone who lucked out getting a teaching job at Harrison in the first place. Now, just 30 years old, I could become a department chair as soon as I relayed the word to the president. Right place, right time. Who knew?

The "interim" status would last through the upcoming second semester of the current academic year, and through the subsequent school year's official search. Short of being arrested for a crime, all signs pointed to the job becoming mine with a five-year contract and tenure to boot.

This would be an opportunity to really shake things up on the sleepy Harrison College campus introducing some faculty

members to the 21st Century. The department chairmanship
came with a spot on the faculty's all-school academic committee, making me one of five voters on course approval or
rejection.

Before phoning my acceptance to President Casey, one more
opinion had to be harvested.

"Holy shit!! Don't be stupid!" That was Mary's immediate
response after we sat down at Whitey's to further discuss this
latest development.

Her second response: "Of course, you say 'yes.' Faculty wait
years for opportunities like this."

Well, yes, but that still left things unresolved between
us, considering she was juggling two job possibilities---Kansas
State and Arizona State---with both separating us.

"Actually, only one, or at least that's the way I'm leaning,"
was her response to this.

And...?

"I like Arizona State," she said. "There'd be less administrative junk, more field work, and interfacing with students,
which I'd like. I don't want to spend all my time in boring committee meetings listening to whiners. I could hit the ground
running at ASU, considering that's where I got my doctorate
and spent summers."

One problem, of course. "I really don't have a firm offer,
like I do from K-State. And I can only hold K-State off so long.
We'd just have to work something out when it comes to us,
I guess.

"Who knows? I could be back at good old Harrison next
year. Might be fun watching you kick a little butt. You will,
won't you? Kick butt."

Definitely, butts needed to be kicked. That was the takeaway
the next day from my call to President Casey to give him my
acceptance. A quick meeting later in the afternoon assured

this would be the case when we went over initiatives he'd like me to advance, and I signed a few papers,

Apparently, he saw me as some sort of conduit with the academic committee, a way to forward his ideas as well as keep him abreast---spy? ---of faculty thinking. "You'll pretty much have carte blanche for matters within the English Department," he said, "but you'll also be in a key spot for advancing other initiatives. We'll work on a budget later."

At the top of President Casey's list?

eSports. He wanted to start a competitive eSports program at Harrison. It would be bolstered by a new course---something to be introduced to the academic committee---that would be part of the school's growing Computer & Communication Department (C&C).

"We've got to get technology moving here," said President Casey. "Nothing can bring us into play quicker than this. It could be a nice jumpstart, a big draw with our new science center."

Left unsaid: a top-notch techy footprint would help the president in his push to build the China connection he coveted. It wasn't my department, but no one from the C&C had a seat on the academic committee.

Gulp. So what are eSports, anyway?

Chapter 29

News Bulletin

"The politics in academia are so vicious because the stakes are so small."
---Henry Kissinger

It did not take long for news from the president's office about the English Department's new, interim chair, me--- Phillip Doyle, to spread. I could only guess at the responses. A barely 30-year old, tenure-less, PhD-less instructor---not even at assistant professor status---becomes a department chair?

A behind-my-back sampling that Mary collected for me:

"Ridiculous choice," according to Dean Brunk to close friends, aghast the appointment got made by a president who went over his head. As Harrison College's dean and chair of academic matters, the high-level classroom staff appointments were to be the group's (his) turf.

"Scandalous," was the echo from Dr. Richard Webber, the fully-tenured history department chair, and academic committee member. As Harrison's library merger initiative rep, he would be in need of the committee's full, low key backing for getting the library decision he desired. Now he could not be sure of this with Doyle and his snoopy band of student writers.

"Who is this Mr. Phillip Doyle person, anyway?" wondered academic committee member Dr. Irena Moldovan, language department chair whose specialties were Latin and Greek. When informed, she deferred to Dean Brunk and followed---as usual---his lead.

Interestingly, there was one positive response. It came from Dr. William Schackelford, the very English Department chair being replaced for health reasons. "We could use a little youthful energy." His remark fell on deaf academic committee ears.

No question I was young for the college's academic committee. By my calculations, the average age of members was somewhere in the low 70s/high 60s. Also, no question its primary exercise was rubber stamping anything on Dean Brunk's agenda to help maintain the school's stagnant status quo.

In my first group gathering, when Dean Brunk introduced me to polite smiles and whispering, the agenda items to be tackled that day included: urging a school holiday (February 9) in honor of college namesake William Harrison, raising the fee paid to visiting classroom speakers, should the writing of Thomas Hobbes (1588-1679) be taught as an offering in politics or English, and whether a history course on the Crimean War needed to be in the curriculum.

Nothing on the agenda was on President Casey's list of initiatives for me to champion when I accepted the department chairmanship. That would come in time. Furthermore, in going over notes from past academic committee meetings, very few decisions and actions came close to his goals for progress into the 21st Century.

Technology? Forget it. Dean Brunk had shown no interest, either in courses for students or workshops to keep faculty compatible with its use. Only a few on the faculty knew more than e-mail. Mostly they relied on department secretaries to keep current in or out of classwork.

Harrison's communications department did not have a seat at this academic table. That meant fat chance for something like an eSport program, which would involve an extracurricular gaming platform and complementary classes. And, as a helpful residual, put us ahead of most small, liberal arts colleges.

After explaining to President Casey the good that could come from involvement, I was sure he'd want me to keep knocking on the door. Over 300 U.S. colleges had adopted eSports teams and small schools like Harrison could be competitive at any level.

All you need is three or four gaming nerds, and you're in business, was how it was explained to me at a conference. Some schools, like Ohio State, UCLA, Purdue, Illinois, Missouri, Utah, and Miami of Ohio gave scholarships and offered majors and minors in gaming technology.

A recognized powerhouse in the sport? Harrisburg University in Pennsylvania, certainly not to be confused with our Harrison College in southern Indiana. For now, anyway.

Chapter 30

What Holiday Break?

It was the start of the second semester, but the holiday break had not been restful. I had to miss Mary's annual family gathering for Christmas skiing in Colorado for the first time in three years. Too many details to get covered before officially starting the new term as chairman of the English Department, if only on an interim basis. I lived in the campus library during the *vacation*. I made it to Whitey's only twice.

Dr. Schackelford was kind enough to invite me to dinner in his home on one of those break nights---but even that turned into a work session. He wanted to go over administrative particulars and early scheduling I would face as his replacement.

Obviously, this was not an easy transition for someone who'd taught 40 years at the same school. We hugged when I exited. I detected a tear in his eye. Who knew if we'd see each other again, and I was lucky to have had his support. I never would forget it.

Fortunately, Bea, his secretary I inherited, was extremely capable. Adding to her growing workload: Her retiring boss had been one of the least capable faculty members with technology.

As he steadily grew weaker from his spreading cancer, her responsibilities grew. It became increasingly obvious she had been running the department in the final weeks.

The lone course I was left to teach---Writing 2--- would become an oasis for me, a refuge from department chair duties. Fortunately, some of my brightest students from Writing 1 and literature classes---Craig Marshall, Tyvonia Braxton, Arthur Graff, Karen Garner--- were on board. This meant we could become even more ambitious in stories for the *Hoosier-Record.* I could cut them loose on independent projects as well as assigned teamwork that would land in the newspaper and be a big help to Newt.

The big surprise when classes resumed? It was extremely gratifying to see Joey Burke among the enrollees. "Good to be back," he said.

Joey had thought his Harrison College days were finished. He dropped out at the start of the year's first term. His parents had suffered a big financial setback and put their farm up for sale. His mother found a job, but that would not cover tuition for both Joey and his sister Brittney.

Nevertheless, Joey, a promising student, had asked to stay abreast of my writing class in the first semester. I sent my syllabus to him, and we shared several lengthy telephone calls going over work assignments that he completed and I perused. They did not receive grades, but easily qualified as "A' work. While he had hopes of someday returning to Harrison, he never thought it would be this soon. He wanted to hit the ground running.

"I'm glad you could make it back," was my greeting. And, with a bit of nosiness on my part, added: "Guess things turned around for your folks."

His smile disappeared. "Yeah, guess that's what happened. I'm living at home, but I didn't want to lose any more ground. I didn't know I'd get back this soon. My brother Jimmy's been a big help."

That was an understatement.

While Joey did not know all the details, big brother Jimmy, one of the better high school athletes to emerge from Harrison County, was enjoying a terrific basketball season at the University of Lexington. The school seemed headed for a conference championship and a possible, first-ever NCAA playoff berth later in March thanks, in good part, to his contributions.

Jimmy came off the Lexington bench several weeks into the season to earn a starting position and lead the team in both scoring and assists. Not only that, but the coach also awarded him a full-ride scholarship. His summer job at the casino would continue on a part-time basis until the end of the current season.

Apparently, it provided enough relief for the parents to temporarily cover college tuition for Jimmy's siblings if they lived at home and commuted. Retaining the family farm was a different matter.

"Jimmy being at the casino is kind of a good thing, too," said Joey. "His job is sort of a no-brainer---a step above maintenance work---but he keeps an eye on things when he's there. He gets some great tips, too."

An eye on "things." It was not that obvious to me or Joey what he meant by "things." I wasn't going to push more in this direction. The look on Joey's face, and the downward glance of his eyes, was a caution sign of sorts.

In bits and pieces in our informal tutorials the past semester, it had come out that Joey's dad, Pete Burke, had a serious gambling problem. Like real serious, as in losing the family farm serious.

The past years had not been especially bountiful for farmers anyway, but Pete, got sucked into thinking he could get it back at the casino. After some modest wins, the losses started piling up. Big time. Before long, he was dipping into savings and, unknown to his wife, Milly, started cashing in the special funds set aside for the kids' tuition.

The last straw? An unexpected visit one night, right after dinner, from two Bel-Tar Casino reps (goons?) with a reminder it was time to start making good on the hole he had dug. Nothing violent, mind you. A schedule of installments was set up to take care of losses---on credit---that had reached the six-figure mark.

No one in the family, except Pete, had the slightest idea what was wrong until the the visitors came knocking. Joey's mom went berserk, crying and yelling at her husband long after Joey, his brother Jimmy, and sister left the house to escape the scene.

In the end, Milly's parents came to the rescue after a strained meeting that saw a tearful Pete, practically on his knees humbling himself, begging for assistance. He got it, forcing his father-in-law to dip heavily into his retirement fund. One final condition written in stone: Pete was to join Gamblers Anonymous and never set foot again in the Princess.

There was an irony that did not escape Milly and her kids. Jimmy's offseason job at the Duchess Casino---the same place Pete piled up losses---took on extra meaning. With his son working in the casino, the dad did not dare set foot on the boat.

The whole, in-depth story would make for compelling newspaper reading, especially in the *Hoosier-Record* with Jimmy being a former local, high school star. This could be touchy territory to enter. This was a writing class, first, and not "investigative" reporting that could prove hurtful.

Still, simply writing about Jimmy's rise to basketball stardom with a NCAA Division 1 program---absent the painful, off-court details---was interesting enough for Newt. The class had not produced a sports story, and this *was* Indiana, where hoops rule.

With brother Joey's consent, Craig Marshall jumped at the opportunity to write the article as an independent project.

Chapter 31

Mr. Clutch

Indeed, Craig Marshall wanted to write the Jimmy Burke story. "Hey, I grew up in Kentucky," he said. "I know you can't miss writing about basketball; especially college hoops."

If Craig had taken a pass, I would have drafted him. There are some students who show actual maturity and he was one--- helped, of course, by the fact he was at least four years older than the rest of the students with a full U.S. Army hitch in intelligence under his belt.

His maturity made it easier to trust him when we informed him of the backstory behind the Burke family's gambling debt woes. This was not to appear in the story---per Newt's guidelines. Sometimes an editor has gotta do what he or she gotta do.

When fully prepped, this was the tale of Jimmy's rise to a starting spot in a Division I basketball program. Frankly, there was enough good material without the ugly back story: The Burke family's descent into massive gambling depths brought on by the father, Pete.

Here was the final, published product:

By Craig Marshall
(Special to the Hoosier-Record)

Jimmy Burke likes a challenge. Harrison High School basket-ball teammates and followers can confirm that.

In Jimmy's senior year playing for the Generals, he was the team's leading scorer and playmaker in a season that included a Southern Indiana Conference championship. This was followed by a post-season tournament run that fell one game short of a highly coveted Class AAA Final Four high school appearance.

"Just three points," he recalled. "We needed just three more points to win that last game against Richardson, and we were in the semifinals. That would've really been something."

While finishing the season with a 30-3 record, including the longest tourney run in Harrison school history, was "something," it's impossible not to wonder how the Generals would've fared with Jimmy on the squad before his senior year.

"I certainly do think about that," laughed General coach Roland Primrose, who retired after that memorable season.

Jimmy had transferred to Harrison, the largest school in the county with an enrollment of approximately 600 students, for his senior season after three successful years with Tippecanoe Consolidated, the smallest school in the county (enrollment: 185).

A leap from Class A's smallest school competition to the big boys in Indiana's next-to-largest Class AAA? No problem.

Just three games into the high school season Jimmy became a General starting guard---and the team never looked back. After losing the opening two games without him as a starter, the team proceeded to win every game with him in the lineup until the ultimate tournament loss. In that stretch, he averaged 23.7 points and 10.2 assists per contest.

In five of those wins, Jimmy scored points in the waning seconds---free throws and three-point baskets---to provide the *victories. "Never saw anything quite like it," said coach Primrose. "He's a winner, no matter what level he plays. Just call him Mr. Clutch. He's got a bright future on and off the court."*

Jimmy Burke hasn't quite made his mark at the next level in college, but he has put himself in position to meet a bigger challenge. After sitting on the University of Lexington bench his first year, he earned a starting spot several contests into his second season.

"I had to be patient," he said, of his entry into NCAA Division 1 competition. "I never considered transferring. I like Lexington. The Thorobreds are on the move, and I want to be part of it."

Lexington has been an NCAA Division 1 program for six years. After a three-year probationary wait, it became eligible for post-season play---though it has yet to qualify for the tournament.

"That's our goal, for sure, the playoffs," declared first-year Coach Whitney Brown. "Jimmy Burke can be a part of that, no question. A big part. He's got all the tools. I'd like to have more Jimmy Burkes."

Brown is in his first year as Lexington's head coach, coming here from an assistant's position at Northeast Texas State. "I liked what I saw of Jimmy in preseason workouts. In addition to being a good outside shooter, he's a real quarterback as a guard. He understood my system from the get-go."

There was this reward with the promotion: With one scholarship left at the start of the season, Coach Brown immediately awarded it to Jimmy, who was a walk-on in that fruitless first season under a different head coach.

The Lexington goal is simple: Make the NCAA Division 1 playoffs for the first time. As a member of the Appalachian Trail Conference, the payoff would be big. The winner of the conference's post-season tournament gets an automatic berth. There's little chance for additional members receiving an independent berth.

"That's our goal, the NCAAs," said Jimmy. "It would be huge for our program."

And, according to Coach Brown, here's one path to take: "If the game's on the line in the final seconds, I want the ball in Jimmy's hands."

Chapter 32

Good & Bad News

Mary's family was the first to know, but that was to be expected. Her offer from Arizona State University arrived on their annual, holiday reunion in Colorado. She had brought her laptop with her for the family ritual, something she normally did not do.

I was in Harrison at the time, organizing my new, larger Durham Hall office to ready myself as the new English Department chair in the upcoming semester. We'd had a few brief calls---her reception was not that good at Rocky Mountain altitudes---but she managed to convey a few details *to* me. Nothing about a decision, but she did confirm she'd received a firm ASU offer.

Did she want her decision to be a surprise? Or had she actually made a firm choice?

While Kansas State wanted her to conceptualize, introduce, administer, and teach courses in her specialty of immigrant migration—with the lure of becoming chair in a department she created, Arizona State simply wanted her to teach and complement it with field work.

Arizona State was where she earned a PhD and was heavily involved in its sociology department's border initiatives in the

U.S. and Mexico. The program was informally known as "Both Sides" as in both sides of the U.S. and Mexican borders.

She'd become an expert on Hispanic migration patterns to the U.S., most notably movement to and settlement, in the upper Midwest and prairie states. She had presented several papers to prestigious, high-profile conferences, both in English and Spanish.

Me? Well, I could operate the manual pencil sharpener in Harrison's English Department.

"So, is it KSU or ASU? Or, neither?" I asked as we sat down to beers at Whitey's. It had only been a few hours since her return to the campus and several days before classes started.

Mary, slowly looking up from her mug, said, "ASU!"

"I just don't see myself as an administrator. That's exactly what that job in Kansas will turn me into. The money is about the same at either place, though I'm sure the cost of living in Manhattan is a lot cheaper."

And the 10,000-pound gorilla in the room left to be addressed was this: What about us?

I was committed to the remainder of this school year and the entire next year at Harrison. Then, I'd learn if the word "acting" would be removed from my title. Hopefully, I'd become the permanent chairman of the English Department with associate professor status.

For me, it was pure serendipity. Further evidence that timing is everything.

"Well, we don't see a whole lot of each other now, and we're in the same apartment building," Mary jokingly countered. "And there are plenty of flights between Indianapolis and Phoenix. I checked. KSU? A long boring trip from southern Indiana by car. Then there are summer breaks and school holidays.

"Look at it this way," she added. "If we were married, big guy, and I know we've talked about this before, we'd be in the same boat. Who gives up their job for the other? We'd both have good situations. I could always stay here and pass up ASU's offer, but I think we both know we'd just be delaying the inevitable. If I stay, what happens if you get a big opportunity elsewhere at some point?"

"No way you should follow me (to Arizona) without a solid job in place."

Hard to argue, especially since I figured to be extra busy in my new role. There'd be twice as many meetings as I already attend. Our time together would shrink no matter what. Of course, with Mary's apartment one floor above mine in the same building, it wasn't exactly like the distance made our hearts grow fonder.

"Let's give this a year, and see what happens," was her answer. "Besides, I haven't told you the good news about the ASU offer. Since I'd want to be doing lots of field work with students, the people I talked to like the idea of establishing some sort of 'in the field' footprint in the Midwest. You know. For hands-on projects.

"My vision is some sort of small space that the school, or a consortium, buys or rents. The school uses it as a base for specific research projects. No reason why I couldn't steer it to southern Indiana. The way Hispanics have energized this area, there's no way some good work couldn't be done in this area. I've already proved that teaching here."

Food for thought that led to burgers and a nightcap at Whitey's before, ahem, dessert back in Mary's apartment.

Chapter 33

Closer Looks

No question the special Harrison library committee learned a lot by the end of their hands-on inspections.

First, they rolled up their sleeves and dug deep into the city's historic, Carnegie-funded public facility, taking a close inspection of everything from holes in the roof to the contents of former head librarian Alva Stone's secret stash.

"Never knew how much there is to a library," said committee member Barney DeWitt. "'Course, gotta admit I never spent that much time in one."

Dr. Webber was seen several more times returning to poke around piles of books carried from Alva's private room. They were stacked up on loading docks behind the library, waiting to be carted away. There was talk of holding a used book sale. Certainly, there'd be no shortage of books to sell. Some could be valuable first editions.

In the case of the college's Grabbe Library, the committee members had to use their imagination. Merging it with the Harrison City Public Library ---plus transferring contents to the campus location---would involve some major, creative remodeling.

The committee visited the Grabbe several times, including one session in which they were presented with detailed illustrations of the project's potential stages. The most obvious transformation would take place in one corner of the first floor, which would become devoted to children. Both libraries were woefully short of material in this department.

"You think anyone will be able to tell them apart from the regular students?" joked Barney---a stab at humor that produced faint smiles.

At least two floors would need a major reconfiguring to accommodate the needs of the new public patrons. "Not much parking space," pointed out committee member Anne Stegora, who showed a knack for finding weak spots during the entire process.

One way or another, everyone agreed money would be an issue. "We're looking at $1 million minimum, you ask me," said Barney.

"At least," countered Dr. Webber.

Keeping the library in its present location certainly would be costly as well. Its needs were imminently expensive and more basic, thanks to those years of neglectful maintenance under Alva. Merging, on the other hand, also meant re-purposing the vacated structure for future use. The city could use the space, but what department would get it?

There also was this undeniable issue looming for the Harrison city library: A head librarian would need to be hired. The salary never was a big issue to Alva, but the city clearly would have to dig deeper into its pocket in hiring her replacement. If Becky Barnes decided to leave, the cost of her replacement also would seriously jack up expenses.

Meanwhile the Grabbe's head librarian, while agreeable to adding responsibilities to her position, would rate a significant raise as a result of a merger. There also would be need for at least one more full-time staffer.

"Damned if we do, damned if we don't," was the way Mayor Tobin succinctly put it. "The money part is almost a wash either way we proceed. An expensive wash, but a wash just the same."

Realizing the final decision could fall in her lap given a committee-city council deadlock, the mayor proposed what seems natural to elected officials. She'd let someone else make the decision.

"We'll call a special election and let constituents decide the library's future," she said.

"We'll make it a county-wide decision, considering this is the only public library in Harrison County."

First, a public hearing would be held with handouts outlining the plusses and minuses of both courses. The vote would take place one week afterward.

Chapter 34

Next Step

The library issue became the talk of the town, fanned in good measure by a series of stories Newt published in his *Hoosier-Record*. "Feels good to do some real reporting for a change," he said.

It was his idea to have my students compile sidebars, stories to complement and add color to the main articles relating to the upcoming election. He would do the lead pieces.

My decision was to have four students work on sidebar stories. They were Craig Marshall, Susan Smith, Karen Garner, and Joey Burke, who, as someone raised in Harrison County, was the lone student to have used both facilities. For them, this was going to be one, giant civics lesson.

"I really want to get everything in the paper Thursday after the Tuesday balloting," Newt explained. "Otherwise, it would be a week later, or almost ten days, following the voting before it gets printed. We've got the website to post news in real time.

"My customers mostly want to see these things in a newspaper they can hold in their hands. It shouldn't be a problem getting the votes counted in time for our deadline. This isn't Arizona. There aren't that many balloting booths in the county. Probably won't be more than a few thousand voters. People love to talk about issues. Getting off their butts and actually voting is another story."

The project figured to give students a taste of real reporting and writing under the gun. Hopefully there would be no challenges to delay things. They needed election officials to get everything counted in time.

A public hearing on the fate of the library issue originally was scheduled for the Harrison City Council chambers. A week before the event, the decision was made to move it to a larger venue---the local Presbyterian Church. Good thing. The unofficial head count indicated several hundred attendees.

"I don't think we got that many for Easter," said the church's senior pastor, Rev. Eugene Kirkpatrick.

This growing interest in the library issue thoroughly amused Becky Barnes, who now was serving as the city's interim head librarian after nearly a decade as Alva's shadow assistant. Where were all these people before this merger question? She could recall days when you could count on one hand the number of library visitors.

The hearing was designed to objectively and publicly reveal detailed plans for the two options---merge or not to merge. In a show of the committee's neutrality, Anne Stegora, long-time Harrison resident, explained at the hearing what would be involved if the municipal library were to be merged into the college's campus. Julie Frank, a committee member and relatively new professor, outlined the necessary updating needed in the community facility if there was no merger.

Some questions and viewpoints were quite valid---costs, taxes, staffing, governance, building upkeep, and hours. Mercifully, the committee dodged a bullet on the subject of book censorship. In a merger and move to the campus, what about books residents might deem inappropriate for young minds? Should there be access? Should there be age limits?

In a pep talk beforehand, Dr. Webber insisted those questions be deferred to him. "I'll just say that is an issue to be determined in the future. Most likely a committee will get formed to set standards."

Ah yes, another committee.

Chapter 35

Start The Presses

The Harrison library story grew into a cash cow for the *Hoosier-Record.*

A week before the special referendum, Newt published an extra section for what he declared a "significant event in Harrison history." He never figured on so many local merchants anxious to buy advertisements---though none publicly committed to one fate or the other for the facility.

Somewhere in this mix, Newt started to lean more on my students for copy. This was a good thing. It gave them a meaningful narrative, deadlines, a need for accuracy, and a conclusion.

In addition to attending meetings, they were assigned to get comments from specific townsfolk to be used in stories. They also administered a special Hoosier-Record website to gather comments from readers. This included weeding out some over-the-top, unfounded remarks from book-ban and anti-library organizations. Lots of cursing, too. It was an education for my guys.

"Whew, there are some angry people out there," said Karen, after working a shift taking telephone calls in the *Hoosier-Record* offices. "I just talked to some guy on the phone who thinks 'The Diary of Anne Frank' should be banned. Can you imagine? Someone that stupid, you gotta wonder if he's even read it."

"I got one the other day saying 'To Kill A Mockingbird' should be banned from all libraries," said Craig. "Probably a racist caller."

"Or sexist. Don't forget the author (Harper Lee) was a woman," countered Karen.

Newt eventually handed over to my students the opportunity to write the lead story in the special section advancing the election. The paper's circulation was only a few thousand readers, but my students---pumped to be a part of this project---treated it like they were working for the *New York Times*. Or at least the *Indianapolis Star*.

This was the result:

Harrison will Take

Historic library Vote!

By Karen Garner, Craig Marshall, Joseph Burke, and Susan Smith
(Special to the Hoosier-Record)

Harrison County residents will get an opportunity in a special referendum next Tuesday and Wednesday to indicate in what direction they want city officials to take for the city's most important, historic institution---the public library.

The ballot, unlike what typically faces voters with dozens of choices, will be simple---only one question. The polls will remain open for two days due to the heightened interest in the question. The popular result is non-binding. The choice:

1, Should the local 110-year old, Andrew Carnegie-founded library remain in its present location? If so, it would undergo a major upgrade that includes an overhaul of its technology, general infrastructure and staffing.

2 - Should the Harrison City Library be moved to the Harrison College campus, where it would be an independent entity with *its own space in the school's Grabbe Library?*

Costs of either move will be comparable, city officials promise. A bond issue would be likely in either development. "We would strive to keep expenses as reasonable as possible," said Mayor Lorna Tobin. "At this point, either option is totally acceptable to the city council."

More details, including sketches, overall funding and infrastructure details are in a special pullout section of this Hoosier-Record newspaper edition. Any Harrison County resident is an eligible voter, but proper ID must be shown to judges. The polling- place locations are listed in today's special section.

"The library's fate is one of the most important decisions in my years in Harrison," said Mayor Tobin. "So important that we're keeping the polls open (8 a.m.-6 p.m.) for two days. We want the community to not miss a chance to have a voice in this matter. This is an informal, but significant, polling of opinions."

The election outcome may be non-binding, noted Tobin, but it will carry significant weight in the Harrison City Council's final decision regarding the library's fate.

Closely watching the outcome will be a special committee appointed by Tobin that's studied and researched the question for several months. The committee is comprised of these Harrison County residents: Dr. Richard Webber, Julie Frank, Anne Stegora, and Barney DeWitt.

The library and its hours have remained intact since the passing of Alva Stone, long-time head librarian, last September. Though short-staffed, Becky Barnes, deputy librarian under Ms. Stone, has kept things running on an interim basis.

"These have been very big shoes to fill," said Becky. "It's an honor to do it, especially leading up to deciding the library's future in years to come. Now it's time to take the needed steps. Libraries are more important than ever.

"One way or another, we need to join the 21st Century!"

Ms. Barnes, like others involved in the transition, would offer no hints of what direction she'd like to see unfold for the library. The committee, according to some, is split 2-2 while the mayor, who has a vote, has been uncharacteristically mum on the subject.

Chapter 36

Library Pulse Beat

"Whew! Our phones haven't stopped ringing," said Newt, taking a seat in our usual booth at *The Dough Girls* coffee and bakery shop.

"I'll have to make this break quick. Amazing, really. I never knew so many people cared about libraries."

Every small town has a place where townsfolk gather for coffee and conversation. In Harrison, it was *The Dough Girls*. Located on the town square, it was operated by two widows, Marge and Millie, who lived above their place of business.

Max, their chief baker, turned out pastry impossible to resist---and without those annoyingly pesky, discouraging calorie counts in display cases. Who really wants to know their chocolate donut with sprinkles has 425 calories when a plain, flavorless bagel has a mere 220?

Customers come from neighboring towns for the cinnamon rolls, though my preference will always be the blueberry scones. The coffee comes with a free refill and, if you're in a hurry, it's in a go-cup. Can it get any better? It's not unusual to see Amish, in their distinct, period-style clothing, standing in line.

At just about any time of the day, there are also healthy portions of gossip to pick up and chew. *The Dough Girls* grist-mill offers a daily weekday menu of topics: politics (local or national), health & aging, sports, economy, schools, weather, deaths, and the media being most popular.

In the days leading to the special referendum, the eatery was busier than usual. Customers had to stand in line much to the annoyance of the regulars. "Just coffee for me, today," declared Newt, taking a seat I'd saved for him. "Busy."

The local library? Pretty sure it never before got discussed over *Dough Girls'* coffee by anyone before the merger issue. The story even got spiked by my students' when the subject first got broached. That's what made this quite a surprise to Newt and me.

No sooner did we take our seats on this day before balloting and Wendell Schmidt hovered over us. He had a question. "What's the deal on this local library situation I read about in your paper?"

"All I know is what I read," said Newt, his standard, smiling response to questions and comments about *Hoosier-Record* content. "It's all pretty much spelled out in the article."

"Looks to me like you left off a third option on the ballot," said Wendell.

"What's that?"

"Do we need a library in the first place?"

This drew a moment of silence and blank stares from both of us before Newt responded. "Really? People here think that? There shouldn't be a library?"

"Sure do, or at least some I've been talking to at church. Waste of taxpayer money. Besides. Ain't that Internet taking its place?"

Newt explained that, as publisher of the local newspaper, it was his responsibility to simply report facts and not take a stand one way or another. The discussion was familiar territory for him. The old "facts matter" argument. He countered beautifully.

"Well, from what I hear, some of them books available are porno. Best way to stop that is not banning books. Just don't have a library."

"Well, I'm sure many people would disagree with what you're saying. The voter turnout will tell us something. But if you think about it, it's kind of difficult to imagine Alva Stone allowing pornographic material in the library."

Wendell answered, "Who's Alva Stone?"

When informed she'd been Harrison's head librarian since the beginning of time, maybe Newt and I should not have been surprised to learn this: Wendell had never graced the local library.

Chapter 37

Victory, Sort Of

Technically there was no such thing as a write-in ballot in Harrison's historic library referendum. In the end, this was a popularity poll asking voters to choose one of two options. No lengthy ballot was filled with unknown people running for obscure offices.

"We'll definitely factor the result into the committee's final recommendation," insisted Mayor Tobin, adding some needed juice to the exercise. "This measure gives more voice to residents in a decision with long-term consequences."

Non-binding or not, the whole exercise was risky for proponents of either of the two options. Several letters to the editor in the *Hoosier-Herald* hinted there was sentiment for no library, or at least pushing for a heavy book-banning hand to be wielded whatever option got followed.

Was this a silent majority that somehow would surface at the polls? Newt didn't publish some of the more scurrilous mail he received but showed me one letter---two full pages of single-spaced vitriol---topped with this line: *"May the wrath of God punish purveyors of filthy untruths!!!!!!!!*

Committee member Dr. Webber was quietly appalled that the public---or "rank and file" as he referred to the general citizenry---could sway the future of such an important literary and factual tool. He did not want the Grabbe to be invaded or picketed by "riff-raff."

"I don't wish to sound arrogant," he said, sounding arrogant. "If our college library does make room for the town's library, there will be direct, open access between the two bodies of citizens. Can townsfolk check out our college-oriented books? Won't this get in the way of faculty, like me, doing serious research?"

Privately, Mayor Tobin let it be known to committee members she was hopeful of a landslide outcome for either option. This would make the committee's recommendation easier to justify, and get her off the hotseat by showing the library was an asset to be valued.

She didn't get it. While there was a record turnout and the outcome favored the merger by 2,211 to 1,993, the city council opted to bow "to the will of the people." The council vote was 4-1 with one abstainer.

Probably because the poll result was not binding, a number of voters were encouraged to scribble a sentence or two on their ballots. Some sentiments were witty and funny, others downright dark. The *Hoosier-Record* ran a few as a sidebar in its post-election coverage.

Here's a sampling:

"Love college library snack bar."

"What nead liberry for!"

"Mayor Tobin's folly?"

"Jesus was certainly literate." Luke 4:16-21

"Enough parking?"

"Don't want my kids near them college students."

"Better programming for local residents?"

"Would be too noisy with both at Grabbe!"

"Beware the wrath of the KKK"

"Screen all porn!"

"Merger mean lower taxes?"
"No overdue fines!"
"Burn all books."
"Need a library book club."

It was not totally unique that a college and municipality shared a library. There were dozens of similar situations according to a check with the U.S. Library Association in Chicago. Furthermore, in a handful of cases, it was an Andrew Carnegie-founded library that gave way to the local college and became re-purposed.

No one had a concrete idea what would become of Harrison's soon-to-be vacated Carnegie structure. Undoubtedly the city, with a major remodeling effort, could use the facility for other municipal business.

The college, on the other hand, was ready to roll with a plan outlined in the *Hoosier-Record's* pre-poll publicity. President Casey, though publicly neutral, was quietly in favor of the merger from the start. For all I knew, it was his idea.

The public library would take over an entire third floor of the college facility which provides a commanding, floor-to-ceiling view of rural landscape.

Under the same roof, the two libraries would operate independently of each other. It would include respective services such as book checkout, acquisitions, budgets, and staffers. The Grabbe would share its auditorium, periodical reading room, tech center, and appropriate programming.

An access card to either library would be honored by both facilities. An escalator connects all floors.

"Maybe we should call it the 'Webber connector,'" joked committee member Anne Stegora, a whispered, behind-the-back jab at the professor. She, like others, had grown steadily weary of the professor's condescending references to community residents.

Everything would be a definite upgrade in resources for the new "city tenant." As expected, the Grabbe books were top-heavy with nonfiction and academic-oriented offerings, but there was a healthy selection of fiction and best-sellers that would overlap with the new neighbors.

"Hey," said Anne, "does that mean if the city library doesn't have a book I want, I can go to the college side---and not leave the same building?"

Yep.

Perhaps the most important adjustment to be made was the city library having more room to expand its selection of material for children and young adults. Hello, *Harry Potter !!*

President Casey and Mayor Tobin held what was labeled a press conference when plans were finalized. The media members attending consisted of Newt, a freelance photographer, my student writers, an intern from the local radio station *WHHR-AM.*

Somehow it all worked. Everything got reported nicely in the press with a modest sprinkling of coverage outside Harrison County. No one could've predicted that the library would generate one more important story that would go "national."

Chapter 38

Digging In

With the "great library decision" behind us and the wheel turned to related details, it was time to get back to my balancing act of teaching an advanced writing class while administering the English Department as interim chairman.

One of my first moves was to check into a raise for Bea, my secretary, who, thankfully, came with the job. Early in my appointment to the faculty, it became obvious that she made the wheels turn as Schack's assistant.

She was appreciative when I informed her of this pay boost, but just as quickly, was handed unrelated paperwork I needed to complete. My pitch for Bea's pay raise sailed through school channels in a flash. (Hey, this chairmanship is going to be fun.)

While Bea made my new duties as painless as possible, she was no substitute for the time I now spent going to meetings, writing reviews, refereeing faculty parking lot space debates, going to more meetings, disciplinary issues and dealing with other complaints that ranged from class scheduling to not enough toilet paper in the restrooms.

"Did I tell you there'd be lots of meetings?" said President Casey, when our paths crossed on the campus mall several weeks into my new responsibilities. Was that a laugh I heard coming from him as we went our separate directions?

Occasionally an entitled student or parent would slip past Bea and reach me directly with some wildly absurd, off-the-wall complaint or looking for a rule-bending move. Students also got to critique professors at the end of a course, with ratings available to the department chair.

This meant I could read my own students' gripes. One favorite: "My professor seemed to Zoom a lot to access experts for us in real-time....and what's the good of that if the expert doesn't come to the classroom?"

Another classic 1: "My professor has the worst wardrobe! It makes it very hard to concentrate on his lectures."

Another classic 2: "The professor calls on us in class to answer questions."

On a more serious note, just a few weeks into my new role there were several cases of plagiarism brought to my attention. These get turned over to a disciplinary committee, but nevertheless require some input from me. The Harrison College rule: Get caught once, you flunk the assignment. Twice? You're on probation. Three times, and it's "hit the road, Jack."

The "Big Kahuna" issues were sexual abuse complaints. Nothing of that sort came across my desk and, truthfully, no one in our English Department faculty seemed comely enough to be a target. To be on the safe side, my advice at the start of each school year was this: When students come to your office for consultation, always, always leave the door open. I did.

The real pleasure for me, in addition to teaching my Writing 2 course, was organizing my Independent Study students and matching them with appropriate feature story projects--- nonfiction or fiction. There were four students in this category.

Each wanted to do nonfiction for the newspaper. More than likely this was because I told them the goal for this *genre* would be getting their work regularly published in the *Hoosier-*

Record. By now Newt welcomed---depended, actually---on getting content from us.

Nothing official, but his circulation had gained at least 150 new subscribers since my students' work began appearing in his publication. "Hard to believe that seems like a big deal, but it is," said Newt. He'd been a star reporter for the Louisville *Courier-Journal* before going "small time" with his purchase of the Harrison newspaper. Before that was a short stint with the Dayton *Daily News* in Ohio.

Furthermore, my students loved seeing their names above stories. An ego thing? Several planned to include their clips in applications to graduate schools after leaving Harrison. "Just like research papers and stuff the professors write for scientific journals," one senior told me. Better, kid. People actually read the students' work when it got published in the local newspaper. Nobody read dissertations.

"Keep it coming," Newt told me one morning over coffee and pastry at *The Dough Girls* when I had broached the subject of our contributions.

"It's win-win. Your stuff from the kids, by the time it gets to me and gets a little editing, is better than I get from my own stringers. They've been a huge help with the library issue."

"Hey, it takes a village," I responded.

The course relief that came with my new status---teaching only one writing class--- figured to make things easier when compared to first semester, when my responsibilities stretched from breaking in new Writing 1 students, shepherding a scattering of Independent Study projects, and teaching a literature course.

Also in the second term, I had more accomplished writers in Writing 2 as well as hand-picked students doubling with Independent Study projects for credit. There would be plenty of room for collaboration among them.

Among my top Independent Project writers:

Craig, the Army veteran, already had proven himself to me with his earlier work. He was good at sniffing out stories, seeing interesting narratives that others might be hesitant to pursue. Also, he was in a hurry to finish work on his degree and return to the military, preferably in intelligence work.

Arthur Graff a nerd, is a computer whiz whose technical knowledge made him invaluable in any field. For sure, it was important to keep reminding him he was writing for audiences that knew little or nothing about computers and technology.

"You're a translator," was my mantra. "You're using words and concepts new to the general public. The faculty, too, as far as that goes."

Danny Newman was a star Harrison College football player from Harrison, a townie who knew local lore. His dad's barber shop, next door to *The Dough Girls* on the town square, was another good place to get current local gossip. And as so often happens in NCAA small-college ranks, Danny was an excellent student---a foreign language major. How many quarterbacks do you find who can call out signals in French?

Karen Garner, from Mishawaka, Indiana, had been valedictorian of her high school graduating class and was well on her way at Harrison to being Phi Beta Kappa. She was an excellent writer. Anyone who knew her had no doubt that someday she would write novels that crack the *New York Times* best-selling lists.

"I prefer fiction," she told me, in an interview to get Independent Study approval. "I'm a big fan of J.K. Rowling (and) what she's done with Harry Potter. I figure more experience in nonfiction, like writing for newspapers, is good background for all writing." Hard to argue.

With this Independent Study crew on board, the second semester classroom figured to be the least of my concerns. As it developed, the public library and its move to the college campus story was just warming up.

Chapter 39

Sorting It Out

Mary and I took our customary booth at Whitey's and had our hands wrapped around our customary bottles of beer, Rolling Rock for her, Miller Lite for me.

Mary was introduced to Rolling Rock, a Pennsylvania-brewed specialty, at a conference she attended in Pittsburgh. Whitey had never heard of it, but, in deference to her, made it an offering. I'm sure he was losing money on it, but ever since winning his establishment's annual 8-ball pool tournament one wintry weekend a few years ago, Mary could do no wrong in his eyes.

He never tired telling me, "You better marry that girl. Quick."

On this particular weeknight early in the second semester, there were few patrons. That was OK. A little privacy was called for this time. We needed to tack down personal matters, namely our immediate futures, without interruptions.

I would be going nowhere for at least another academic year, which would see me fulfilling my role as interim English Department chair. If all went well, this would be followed with a five-year contract with tenure status as the permanent department chair.

A chair at the college's leadership table? Heady stuff for someone barely more than 30 years old. I'm positive some of my old teachers would turn in their graves over this news. For sure it would roast current, stuffed-shirt colleagues.

"You had to take it," said Mary. "You wouldn't have to remain at Harrison after five years. You'd have a lot of options with a chairmanship on your resume. You could go either the academic or administrative routes. I know people better qualified with PhDs who spent their whole academic career waiting for something like this---and it never happened."

Gee, thanks. I wasn't exactly sure how to take her remark. Was she trying to shed me? Mary could be pretty blunt about things. Before I could respond, she immediately added: "But taking it doesn't mean we get separated." Whew.

But this was the easy topic on this night. Now that Mary was headed for Arizona State the next academic year, we had come to another intersection. Our personal lives.

Mary, showing some relief, said she would let Kansas State know tomorrow that, while she appreciated the offer, she was headed to ASU. That aside, now it was obvious she wanted to talk some more "about us," meaning our future together.

Now the big question was this: How do we handle the separation? Or do we handle it, pull the plug, and just let our relationship die a slow death? What IS our status, anyway? It was true we did not spend all that much time together during the school year. Would my new position mean even less time?

"I think we'll get a good idea by the end of this semester," she said. "Think about it. You'll have almost the same workload for the foreseeable future at Harrison. Me, too, at ASU. Maybe we just wait and see, and make some decisions at the end of this year."

My response, "What decisions? That's the question. We'll probably know then what we know now."

At this point---probably to the relief of both of us---Whitey walked over and plopped down in our booth.

"So. How's my favorite coo-some two-some tonight?" he asked.

Said Mary: "You keep offering Rolling Rock (and) you'll always have at least one customer. Me. None of that pedestrian stuff like Miller Lite."

After taking a look around, she added: "Things are kind of quiet tonight. Where's everyone? We haven't been here for a while; usually there's at least one card game going."

Drawing a quick frown from Whitey, he explained business had been slow for at least a month or so. This was especially unusual for the winter, when most of his crowd didn't like being outside in the cold unless they were ice fishing.

"This winter's going to be bad," he said. "I dunno. Maybe it's time for me to think of selling and retiring."

We'd heard this before from Whitey. Now he sounded a shade more resolute. Sad, too, but definitely resolute. The problem, he was convinced, was the Princess Casino's more aggressive marketing with added gaming formats. He was taking it personal, too.

"Hard to compete with something like that being in your backyard," he said. "It's the sports betting. Now that you can do it legally on that boat, well, it's a big draw. I never saw it coming.

"Hell, I had guys making bets in my place all the time but that was different. It was all informal. Fun. Illegal, but informal. Nobody I heard of ever got into it too deep.

"But that damned boat is sneaky. They keep their booze prices low. Lower than me in some cases. When customers get liquored up, they bet more. That's how they make their nut. Ever hear of anyone really hitting it big with a bet? Not me."

Whitey's diatribe went on for a few more minutes. We'd never heard him rant quite like this.

"You want to know the worst thing about this?" he continued. "I hear all kinds of stories of people becoming big losers. I mean big. We don't get a savvy sports crowd here. Losing their farm, that sort of thing. They may follow it closely and then put their money on the locals---Colts, Pacers, IU, Purdue, Notre Dame, Kentucky, whatever. You name it.

"They're quick to tell you about a big win when it happens. Ever notice nobody talks about how much they lost?

"I suppose it makes me kind of hypocritical, since I'm in the hospitality business. But I always cut a customer off if I think he had too much to drink; you know, before he did something really stupid. The way I hear it, at the Princess, they just keep pouring it down the customers. What do they care? The owners don't live here. They probably live in Detroit or some other distant town."

We'd never seen Whitey worked up quite like this, his face turning a deeper red than normal. It definitely tossed cold water on our conversation---the part in which we'd get more intimate and discuss the future as a couple. There was time for that later.

The next order of business, we agreed, would be Mary officially declining the Kansas State offer. Me? One item in Whitey's harangue that caught my attention. According to him, a Gamblers Anonymous group was getting off the ground somewhere in Harrison County. Its weeknight meetings were held in a church basement.

"Pretty bad when that happens; tells you something, like how bad it's getting," said Whitey, referring to this news. "Their meetings are pretty hush-hush, but I heard already there are some horrible stories. People who can't afford to get in deep at the Princess. Sad stuff. That never happened before sports betting became legal in Indiana."

While the next day Mary would be calling Kansas State, my schedule would include a call to Newt. Did he know about

Gamblers Anonymous opening a chapter in Harrison? Maybe he would publish a story? Or would that be too deep for my students?

Chapter 40

Beating The Odds

It was wintertime, but the room in the Methodist Church basement in Harrison's outskirts on this weeknight was hot, stuffy, and overcrowded. The gathering was ten minutes late getting started as Barry, the organizer and facilitator, and his assistant, Jeff, scurried into an adjacent storeroom to find more folding chairs.

There were 24 people attending Harrison's introductory Gamblers Anonymous meeting. No one knew what kind of turnout to expect. To everyone's knowledge there never had been a GA chapter in the community, or anything close to it. This had to be concrete evidence---dubious as it was, that the nearby Princess had "arrived."

There could be no question that traffic on the boat kicked up a notch with the arrival of legal sports betting. Pete Stanley, who'd managed the operation since the day one opening nine years ago, couldn't get over arriving for work at 7 a.m. on week-days only to find lines of customers waiting for doors to open. Are these people nuts, he'd think. Depressing.

On the other hand, maybe this was predictable. The gambling industry had taken over sports at almost every level. The NCAA had sold out, thought Pete. So-called amateur athletes were in line to get paid from a variety of sources, nefarious or not. And all sorts of other rules were loosened---meaning every fumble, dropped fly ball, and missed free throw on playing fields could be questioned by bettors and fans alike: Were the athletes on the take?

Yes, but how could that be happening if celebrities such as Peyton Manning, Halle Berry and Ben Affleck say casinos are the place to be?

Well, for starters the gambling and sports industry were legally in bed with TV, at least a billion dollars passing hands annually on advertising and marketing alone. More sportscasters worked betting and other favorable references in commentary and news reports, adding an air of legitimacy to this marriage. Casinos were within walking distance of most major sports stadiums.

Perhaps it was totally predictable a GA chapter would follow (if there hadn't been one already) in this location. They were sprouting like dandelions in the spring everywhere else.

Nothing like Notre Dame vs. Alabama in football to get juices flowing. Or Kentucky vs. Louisville in basketball. All it took was winning one bet to make ten more. TV told schools when to schedule contests.

It was obvious---judging by license plates in the church parking lot---gambling fever had landed in downstate Illinois, Kentucky, Ohio and southern Indiana---states that in the past were slow, or forbidden, to offer gaming.

For many GA members, it could be embarrassing to have neighbors learn they had a gambling problem. Undoubtedly there would be dropouts; there always were. But there never was a shortage of GA prospects to take their place.

Judging by the makeup of this first meeting, the gambling bug cut a wide path. Those vehicles in the parking lot ranged from showy BMWs to mud-splattered pickup trucks with over

100,000 miles on odometers. One brave soul rode a motorcycle despite temperatures in the high 20s.

This inaugural session also would be Barry's first chapter leadership role. A reformed gambler himself (a pre-requisite to this unpaid position), he had assisted with meetings in a dozen or so established chapters throughout the upper Midwest. He considered it a full-time job. Never mind that he was only 41 years old.

A former commodities trader in Chicago, Barry (only first names get used in and out of meetings) struck it rich early in his career. Soybeans had been very, very good to him though he'd never set foot on a farm in his life. Action in the trading pits became no different than a six-figure wager on Clemson over Southern Cal by at least 5 points---and watching the game become a see-saw affair on TV. College football and hoops became Barry's betting passion.

"I could live with that pressure, but I bent too many Board of Trade rules feeding my habit," he said. "Lost my trading license. What next? My wife threatened to leave, take the kids with her. She went back to her old job teaching school. We were getting the bills paid, so we were lucky from that standpoint.

"College tuitions are down the road. That'll be a problem. My story's really not much different from what I hear at our meetings. No matter what develops on the job front, I'll stay involved in some way with Gamblers Anonymous. It's therapy for me too."

His initial Harrison turnout was what Barry expected: blue collar, white collar, young, old, white, Black, male, female; everyone sneaking peeks at each other to see if there were any familiar faces. Most had a good idea of the format---discussing their gambling history in front of strangers---from watching meetings on TV dramas.

At the start, Barry laid down rules:

**First names only.

**What happens and gets said at meetings stays at meetings (no recording devices, photos).

**Refrain from using dollar amounts in conversations.

**No borrowing or lending of money to fellow GA members.

**Do not mention crimes you still may be prosecuted for.

Barry counted on turnover, a steady flow of newcomers replacing quitters. From his vantage point, gamblers with a problem were a growth industry. Some would leave out of shyness, dropping out after their first session. That would be especially true if someone else they knew was also in attendance. Some newcomers would be annoyingly windy telling their stories. Barry knew all the cues, could cut them off.... ever so politely. It was an art.

For some participants, expressing feelings in front of strangers was painful. It took several sessions to warm up to the concept. For others, it was a cathartic experience that brought them relief you could see in their expressions.

The demographics? Middle-aged men, like their meeting leader, outnumbered others. There was a half-dozen women at this gathering, a little less than a third of the turnout. This was a tad high, but too early in the process to make judgments.

"It's rare that you see older people, like in their 70s, even 80s, but it happens," said Barry. "If they had a gambling problem, it usually started at a younger age and they'd be tapped out before getting old...or they'd committed suicide, and I'm not kidding about that."

No, he wasn't kidding. Suicides always were a concern--- gambling's dirty little secret.

It is not unusual that they occur in casinos, a panicky loser walking from a big loss at the poker table directly to a restroom where he or she jumps from a window. Look closely, and some of the newer casinos are built without windows above the first floor or, in some cases, with restraining safeguards.

The gambling-linked suicide rate has been on a steady climb as access grows. Gamblers aren't limited anymore to Nevada or Atlantic City for enticing settings. From slot machines in gas stations to celebrities touting the "excitement and thrill" of casinos, obsessive wagering is better than a billion-dollar, inescapable industry.

There always were first-timers at GA meetings, convinced they did not have a gambling problem. They were participating merely to mollify a spouse or other loved one. Besides, you might even pick up a betting tip or two.

This inaugural meeting had Barry tossing out questions for discussion and, much to his satisfaction, they sparked lively responses. It was a good start.

A sampling from participants:

1- Has gambling ever made your home life unhappy?

"My wife divorced me, took the kids. Lost all our savings for their college tuitions. What do you think? Unhappy would be putting it mildly."

2- Did you ever borrow to finance your gambling?

"I went through bankruptcy---twice. Couldn't stay away from the tables. High stakes poker. I found a friendly banker the second go-round. I was told he got fired soon after I filed again."

3- After a win that exceeded your goal, did you have a strong urge to continue gambling?

"Are you kidding? Of course. Who wants to go home when you're on a streak."

"Try this. Up $10,000, then down $15,000. I kept telling myself: I can get it back if I already did it once."

4- Did you ever lose time from work or school due to gambling?

"Not really; but just ask me how many times I went to work on little or no sleep."

5- Have you ever sold something to finance your gambling?

"Wedding ring. Thought I could win it back at the table. Never did."

"My grandfather's Purple Heart medal from the Korean War. He was senile at the time, so I figured it was worthless to him."

At this first GA session in Harrison, four attendees were in their early 20s. Young adults. That demographic was increasing as well.

"I say technology is the door opener for them," Barry explained. "It's such an easy segue from online gaming---especially poker. I can name several schools that have gaming devices in the student unions and dormitory lounges."

On the other hand, Barry acknowledged, it was dangerous to pigeon-hole or typecast those attending GA meetings. For instance, he was unaware one attendee who never missed a meeting for several years was a Catholic priest---sans collar. He still wouldn't know this if the good padre hadn't been arrested for cooking the books at his church---presumably to pay gambling debts.

They heard from a former policeman who became so consumed by gambling that he took bribes to support his habit. Eventually, he was caught, arrested, served six months in jail, lost his job and the benefits he'd accrued after 23 years on the force.

"I never paid back a lot I borrowed including from my own son...," he said. "I had to make up a lot of excuses. I'll never forget the day I was arrested. I fainted."

Sheila didn't faint when she was arrested for embezzling to support her gambling, though she stole money from the charitable organization she headed.

"I know this has to be about as low as it gets," she said. "Playing the slots was like having a frontal lobotomy. You sit there and you listen to the music and, I dunno, it's like something cares, but that's ridiculous. It's just a machine.

"I served a year in prison. It was so humiliating. I wouldn't let my kids visit me. We moved to another state to start a new life. I don't gamble anymore or haven't for three and a half years, but I keep coming to these sessions to stay strong."

One thing Barry knew for sure about his newly-formed chapter. There would be many more heartbreaking testimonies and plenty of tears down the road. Surprises, too.

Chapter 41

Family Reunion

It was a rare experience for the Burke boys. There were few opportunities to get together like this during the school year.

The University of Lexington basketball schedule made it almost impossible for Joey to schedule a trip, three hours each way on Interstate 64, to watch older brother Jimmy compete.

Even the Christmas holiday, a traditional feel-good break in everyone's routines, was filled with practices and a holiday hoops tournament. Little time was left for personal pleasure and reunions.

Lexington, or UL, was in the big time now. The Thorobreds were way out of Harrison's small-school class. Having moved up to NCAA Division 1 ranks only a few seasons ago, this meant more long-distance road games and, in general, little free time from mid-October to April. The players had tutors to help with classroom work; practices and travel were the back-breakers.

A home game on Saturday afternoon in Lexington against a lesser foe, Clarksville State, gave Joey just enough time to squeeze in his first game of the season to watch his brother compete. He was having a good season. Not coincidentally, so was his team. They won this game easily.

Miraculously Joey's car, a 2011 Hyundai Sonata with 104,000 miles on it, held up. Now, an hour after the contest's final horn, the brothers sat in a Waffle House booth just off I-64 on Lexington's west edge.

"Great game," said Joey. "Great seat to watch it, too. Thanks. Right behind your bench. Got to say, your coach (Whitney Brown) gets into it."

Lexington never trailed in the contest, beating Clarksville 88-74. Jimmy was his team's leading scorer for the young season, though his 12 points in this contest were significantly lower than his average.

He did have 13 assists and, even to a novice fan, it was obvious he controlled the game's pace for his team. "This was a breather," said the older brother, Jimmy. "Games will start getting tougher down the stretch. We think we got a shot at getting into the NCAA tournament."

The Thorobreds would've been a heavy betting favorite in this game, but, since its opponent was a smaller Division II opponent, the contest was scratched off official sportsbook charts by oddsmakers for lack of interest. Only Division I programs playing each other get the "honor" of being formal betting targets.

"Too bad," said Jimmy. "Someone could've hit it big if they knew how to play a point spread. I could've set 'em up."

This wasn't exactly what Joey wanted to hear. His basketball-playing brother's summer job working at the Duchess, a casino in Bel-Tar's fleet with the Princess and two other boats, obviously had opened his eyes to the gambling world, its vocabulary and personnel. Terms and words such as "the line, over-and-under, double down, point spreads, slots, odds" and "oddsmakers" were popping up almost too easily in his conversations.

"I like Coach Brown," Jimmy continued. "He's been good to me. Jacking up my scholarship to a full-ride this year was huge given the problems Dad and Mom are having. You know that as well as I do.

"How *are* things at home with the folks anyway?" he quickly added. "I've sort of lost touch; basketball has kept me busy. Things sort of fall on your shoulders living at home. Sorry about that, too."

Joey brought his brother up to speed. The big news was that their father no longer owned the family farm. The bank, after numerous warnings, finally foreclosed, took it back, and promptly put it on the market. The family could stay in the house until a sale was in the works.

"That's bad, really bad," said Jimmy, with a quick frown.

Meanwhile, their father, Pete, had taken a full-time job at the turkey processing plant---where Joey worked full-time in the summer and part-time now that he had returned to Harrison College.

"It's a little embarrassing for Dad when our paths cross at the turkey plant," said Joey. "Doesn't happen very often, though. I'm just part-time."

"Yeah. Got to be humiliating if you ask me," responded Jimmy. "I'd like to do more to help. Gotta be some way I can help."

Joey went on to explain their dad purposely asked for the night shift (5 p.m.-midnight) at the plant. It paid better and created more daylight hours for him to make a few bucks on the side. The downer: he couldn't follow his son's basketball games.

"Dad still does some part-time stuff on the farm while the bank looks for buyers," he added. "What a downer, shoveling cow shit and gathering eggs and other things like that on a place you once owned."

"Maybe he'll do some spring plowing," said Jimmy. "That'd be a step up."

The goal, according to Joey, was to keep their father busy and accountable 24/7. Not just to work, but to keep his mind off gambling. With a son doing so well in college sports, he'd love to be at the games---but that atmosphere could be counter-productive!

Also, and this was news to Jimmy, their father was attending Gamblers Anonymous (GA) meetings on Sunday night in Harrison. Their mother was driving him to sessions and waited in the parking lot for meetings to end. For Milly, this wasn't much different than sitting in the car and watching Jimmy and Joey play Little League baseball and youth soccer.

"One thing. I'm getting a lot of reading done," she told Joey, allowing herself a rare sliver of humor.

"Man, that's bad," said Jimmy. "That GA stuff is for real sick-o's. I heard about it last summer when I was working at the casino. Dad definitely got in deep shit. I didn't realize how deep until now. Minimum six figures. Unbelievable. Let's hope he's turned the corner. Sure wouldn't want him betting on my games. That's pressure I don't need."

He added, "I guess it's up to us to keep helping. You live at home and work part-time. Sis transfers to a cheaper school. I guess my contribution is my basketball scholarship. I'd like to do more. Next summer I've been promised another casino job with Bel-Tar on one of their boats. I get a pay raise, too. That'll help."

Joey got home safely from the Lexington game. His Hyundai held up, and he got the usual 34 miles per gallon on the clunker. Thank goodness he didn't have a gas-burner. Buying another car---used and for sure cheap---would be out of the question at this family low point.

In fact, just about every expense outside of food and rent was out of the question. Jimmy was right. Pete did get them into a deep hole. Milly was already worried about the summer months ahead, when her job as a cook at the high school would be put on hiatus. Maybe she could find something at the college, working something comparable at summer camps that take place on the campus.

The more Joey thought about it while driving back to Harrison, one thing seemed to be creeping into the picture: brother Jimmy's growing bond with Bel-Tar. How close was it? Where was that headed? His growing knowledge of the gambling industry was one thing. His admiration for those in the industry was quite another.

Maybe I'm imagining something, Joey told himself. I sure hope so.

Chapter 42

Here Comes the Parade

There never was a day like this in the 175 years of Harrison College history. Or for that matter, the 130-year history of Harrison's municipal library.

Now that the infrastructure work was nearly completed, and technological resources were in place, the transfer of the old Harrison Public Library books and other resources were ready to make the move to the remodeled first floor of the Grabbe Library.

The Old Carnegie doors would permanently close as the library would await its fate. Current speculation, according to the *Hoosier-Record,* had it converted to offices for the mayor, city clerk, and city council chambers. The local chamber of commerce also was known to be lobbying for space.

"It'll take a long time not to think about the building as a library," said Mayor Tobin. "Old Alva would be turning over in her grave ... If she hadn't been cremated."

What happens to approximately 30,000 books? That's what needed to be carted to the Grabbe, a number pared to that figure from 40,000 by eliminating unneeded duplication.

In a stroke of genius, someone (my money's on President Casey came up with this brilliant idea: Instead of hiring an expensive trucking service with paid movers, volunteers would be organized from all parts of Harrison to make it a hand-carried transfer! After all, the two buildings were within easy walking distance of each other.

"We'll make it a real town and gown experience," the president said. The college's athletic teams pitched in as well as representatives from other extracurricular groups such as mock trial, Model U.N., music, foreign language clubs and drama.

Locals? Three church groups, several public school teachers, most of the city council, three book clubs, members of the high school's soccer teams, and a half dozen full-time first responders volunteered to join the procession and carry loads.

The Grabbe was only six blocks away from the Old Carnegie. The mayor would sign an official proclamation on the Carnegie steps turning the day into an official, local holiday. Volunteers were then handed what they could carry at the Carnegie and formed a line headed for the campus, where more volunteers waited at the dock for the handoff and registration.

What started as a simple idea morphed into an "event." It took on the appearance of a festive homecoming parade or, better yet, a small, literary Mardi Gras. Some helpers wore costumes, others pulled toy wagons loaded with books, at least three volunteers wore tuxedos, the women's basketball team wore their warmup jackets, a platoon of volunteer firemen dressed in their gear, and one couple rode horses. Musical instruments included two bag pipers, three trumpet players and a drummer.

Several local businesses had entries in the book parade. The city's funeral home, Piedmont Burial & Cremation Services, stole the show. Four young men in suits serving as "pall-bearers," carried an open casket filled with a hundred volumes.

The Dough Girls provided coffee, soft drinks, and baked goods on the Grabbe steps.

The local Wal-Mart pitched in with "official" cloth bags to be filled with books. The date, city seal, and a special logo were prominently stamped on the book bags, which were given away at the end of the day. Everyone got a library card if they did not already have one.

Fortunately, it did not rain despite a gloomy forecast.

Since the event was on a weekend, Newt went big on pictures that would not appear in the *Hoosier-Record* for almost a week. While he hated getting "scooped" by outsiders, especially in his own city, the delay gave him extra time to create a special section with extra photos. This was another cash cow for him, too. The main headline in big, bold type read, "Turning The Page."

The daily Evansville *Courier & Press* sent a reporter and photographer for a big splash under the headline, "Book Ends!" The Associated Press circulated a photo, which was picked up in the *Indianapolis Star's* state edition. Two of my independent study students wrote sidebar stories to go in Newt's weekly with his lead story and two photo pages.

Joey Burke practically begged me to participate. He wanted to write a first-person account of the transfer. He was one of the few Harrison College students who, as a townie, used the community library. It would be a first-person account.

Good angle, good story, said Joey. How would it feel to see his hometown library gutted? This was where he and his siblings learned and read under the watchful eye of Miss Alva. We didn't know then, but his story would later win several statewide journalism awards.

The first paragraph of his feature certainly was a winner:

"For me, this was the final chapter. Literally."

The books and other materials that didn't make a final cut were left in the Old Carnegie. Every volunteer who helped was allowed to grab an armful for themselves in "payment" for their labor. This helped pare the pile. A used book sale was organized for the following week. Anything remaining following that would be donated to public schools throughout the county as well as additional social service institutions.

Joey was one of the few to grab an armload. He did it carefully, for old times' sake. He selected several children's books he recalled reading. Then he worked his way up the ladder to *Hardy Boys* mysteries and eventually several Harry Potter's. Just for good measure, he grabbed several biographies that he hoped were valuable first editions.

Chapter 43

Call Him Curious

With the library issue well on its way to being solved, college life settled down and my Durham Hall office door remained open to students, especially if they'd made an appointment. Typically, only a small trickle took advantage of this in the early weeks of a new semester, particularly timid freshmen. Walk-ins were also welcome.

As the semester progressed, and for sure if a decent grade looked to be in jeopardy, my office traffic got busier with final exams nearing.

Though she never said it outright, Bea gave me every indication students visiting the office were a bit of a rarity. This almost never happened in Dr. Schackelford's later years. She stopped short of making any judgments, but it was obvious she approved of my open door and the rapport this built.

"It's always nice for me to match faces with a name," she said. "Some of these kids make me feel like I'm their mother."

As I got to know students, it was not unusual to learn many had at least one good story to write from something they'd experienced or knew. Some had enough first-hand material for a book. Such had to be the case with the Ukrainian (Faddei) and Mexican (Arturo) refugee students who sat side-by-side in my Writing 1 class. Their border crossings had to be more challenging than driving I-80 from Illinois into Indiana.

I hoped to learn more about the challenges faced by these two, which most likely would make excellent *Hoosier-Record* material. Since they were in special counseling programs with a tutor at Harrison, I never asked and, unless special guidelines got passed down to me, I treated them no differently than if they were from Kokomo or Greencastle.

It was not unusual to have high-profile headlines and celebrity connections play out in some tangential manner on the Harrison campus. Maybe not all that direct, but something that still might have a place in an essay or feature story.

One classic was a student of mine whose father attended a private prep school in Switzerland at the same time as Kim Jong-Un, who became North Korea's dictator.

"My Dad sat next to him in a math class. He said he was kind of a chubby guy the students made fun of. They nicknamed him 'Buns.' He pretty much stuck to himself, but he smiled a lot. He always had a security guy with him."

Former Vice President Mike Pence's grandnephew was a student at Harrison. Well, sure, the Veep's relatives had to attend school somewhere, except in this case, the lad happened to be president of the campus chapter of Young Democrats.

That goofy little Leprechaun mascot at Notre Dame athletic events? The one that works at keeping Fighting Irish fans jazzed at football contests in South Bend? For over 50 years, it was always a male student until a few years ago, when after annual tryouts, a coed was selected who happened to be the older sister of one of my students.

My own brush with fame: a daughter of Steven Tyler, the rabid-like lead singer for Aerosmith's rock band, was a classmate of mine at my college undergrad alma mater. Very few knew this, including me, until she talked Pops into singing the Star-Spangled Banner for a Parent's Weekend football contest---a performance no one who witnessed will ever forget.

"Connect the dots," I would tell my writing classes. "Be alert. Dig up enough dots to connect and the story writes itself. Just follow a few structural steps to organize the content around a narrative. Hopefully, you'll learn them in my class."

Nosey. Curious. Thorough. Well-read. Know your audience. Those were some of the traits that made for good writers. We worked at them throughout the semester. And it's always easier, at the start, to stay in familiar territory, like the jock, male or female, writing about a sports highlight, a music major writing about a concert, or an anthropology major writing about a dinosaur dig.

One student who understood this---and was a welcome, frequent office drop-in who brought coffee---was Craig Marshall. Following four years in the U.S. Army's intelligence wing, he was wise beyond his years.

Being over 21 years old, he could go places many of his fellow students were not allowed. His maturity and mobility gave him perspective. His nosiness fueled his imagination. On one visit, he told me a story that definitely could have some meaning.

"One night in the Princess, I saw these four tall, slender teens or early 20s come out of the boat manager's office," he said. "Their expressions were on the serious side, tight-lipped. It was a few minutes past midnight.

"Kind of weird, really. I probably wouldn't have noticed, but they were so tall. They just seemed out of place. I felt like following them but didn't. What do you think?"

Well, it did sound interesting ... even by casino standards, where you figured to see all sorts of strange sights at any hour. First, I was curious to learn what Craig was doing in the Princess that late.

I knew he wanted to do an ambitious writing project about the boat---who frequents it, interviews with big winners and losers, chat things up with dealers, and trace its economic impact on the area.

Business was booming at all hours, especially with sports betting now legal in Indiana and not-so across the Ohio River in Kentucky and Ohio. That made the Princess the only casino with legal sports gaming in Bel-Tar's fleet of four. The local TV advertising made viewers believe the Princess was another Caesar's Palace in Las Vegas.

Undoubtedly there would be a lot of *Hoosier-Record* readers interested in what takes place in the casinos that almost never close and are only a stone's throw from the campus. Any casino stories by my students would have to be a highwire act, though, if not handled correctly. There'd be a good chance Newt would give a thumbs-down to the idea. The last thing he needed was a libel suit, or, possibly worse, the casino might pull lucrative advertising out of his publication.

Craig, not a regular *Hoosier-Record* employee, would be vulnerable like the college itself. Now that I was a department chair, I'd have to monitor his efforts closely. On the other hand, this could lead to a well-read article, something to get away from the "soft" stuff we had been producing for the weekly. Might even win a few prizes.

Everything sounded like Craig was off to a good start. At this point, he'd earned my trust. As far as I was concerned, he had a free hand to pursue what angle interested him, then he would get back to me with his first draft. I would reserve judgment until I saw it. He'd need to be careful, keep it local, entertaining, and above board while taking readers into a new world.

No question the Princess Casino was an economic engine in southern Indiana that was growing fast. There were over 100 full-time employees, topped in the region only by our turkey processing plant. Rumor had it that Bel-Tar owners in Detroit already had expansion plans on the drawing board. It included building an adjacent hotel.

How deep did Craig want to dig?

It turns out he'd spent several nights cruising the casino premises until 3 a.m., when Princess gaming got down to a handful of hard-core poker games and a few slot machines.

"Guess I'm just curious," he told me. "Thinking of something like 24 hours in the life of a casino. Think that'd work?"

The writing would have to be colorful and straight forward, at the same time, it shouldn't be a problem. Newt could always have his newspaper's lawyer go over the final version. The boat management probably wouldn't allow photographs.

This might be a good project for fellow student Karen Garner to join, considering her writing skills were excellent. They'd need to keep a low profile. The story would need a touch of creativity, but heavy with provable facts.

Craig discovered the busiest spot in the tell-tale late hours generally was the coffee shop, where hard-core gamblers had early breakfast or a late snack. Some patrons came from far distances, and there weren't places to eat before they drove home. That's why a hotel was in the plans. Keep the bettors close to their imaginary pot of gold.

Other customers arrived early in the morning---before they punched a clock at their job. "Lines of people at 6 o'clock in the morning. Some people really got the fever bad," Craig told me.

By looks on their faces, he added, you could easily tell winners from losers. It could be a grim scene.

To Craig, especially depressing was the occasional glimpse of parents with a school-age child napping in his or her lap on a school night while Mom or Dad fed a slot machine.

It was not unusual to see a customer off in a corner, on the phone begging for a quick loan from a pal. Tempers could run short in the coffee shop, especially if customers sitting near each other had been in the same poker game.

"Once, I helped break up a fistfight," Craig told me. "One guy wouldn't tell the other player what he was holding in an unchallenged, winning Poker hand.

"Another time I was asked by a big winner to follow him into the parking lot. He was scared he was going to get jumped on the way to his car. Some real sights, colorful. Kinda like a police blotter coming alive. Karen's a better writer than me. She'd be perfect to work with on this.

"Yeah, I've even seen a few from the college trying their hands at some payoffs, usually at the poker table."

"Students, right?" I asked.

"Well, not all," he told me. "I've seen a few I think are profs here at the college."

Now that was interesting.

Chapter 44

Jackpot!!

Now that he was enrolled again as a full-time student, Joey Burke also became a more frequent visitor in my Durham Hall office. Living at home meant he didn't have a dormitory room on campus as an oasis.

My digs became a sort of landing strip for him, a residual from his visits when he was not enrolled as a student the previous semester. In those dark days for him in the first term, he wanted to stay abreast of what was taking place in my classroom. Imagine that.

We became buddies. Nice kid. Occasionally Bea found odd jobs for him. If I wasn't too busy, we'd have a lengthy chat. I liked this; good way to find out what students were thinking.

Joey, as a townie, had unique access to both community and campus gossip. In the short time I'd been teaching, I always appreciated having a student like Joey; hard worker, punctual, savvy, a good listener who looked you in the eye during a conversation.

He'd probably never win a Pulitzer, but he did appreciate my sense of humor. The surest way to any professor's heart was to laugh at his or her jokes.

With Joey, I was becoming some sort of father figure. And, in piecing together bits and segments in our chats, things were not going so well in the parental portion of the Burke household. He could use another father figure.

"My Dad doesn't seem to be doing well," said Joey. "Something's not right. He's always a lot quieter, sort of mopey. He and Mom argue a lot. And I mean a lot. When they see me starting to listen, they hush up----but I know things aren't right. Pretty sure it's got something to do with money."

Not until halfway through the semester would I start to get a clearer sniff of Burke family troubles. It came following a class as I was filling my briefcase. I looked up to see Joey lingering at the door.

"Joey, you haven't dropped by my office for a while. Where have you been hiding lately? Bea's been saving some tasks for you."

"Sort of busy," was his response at the time. "I've got a new, part-time job taking up a lot of my time."

"Something interesting, I hope."

Not exactly, it turned out, unless you were into packaging turkeys on an assembly line in a stifling, hot warehouse. He worked weekends, plus two separate, part-time nighttime shifts in the county's turkey processing plant. This left no time for leisurely chats with a professor---me---or little else except keeping his head above water in schoolwork.

Over time I would learn the Burke household had become a shambles.

Pete, the father, was a hopelessly addicted gambler. As a result, he had fallen so far behind in his mortgage payments the local Harrison bank was in the process of foreclosure. He had literally gambled away the family farm at the Princess Casino.

Several of the assignments Joey completed required him to miss three part-time shifts, money sorely needed in the household. When I learned this, I felt bad. I made a mental note: Make adjustments for Joey.

"We can stay on it until it gets sold," Joey told me, "but that's it. The value of the crops at that point gets applied to what we owe, or something like that. I just hope to stay in school. My sister, too. Jimmy's lucky with his basketball scholarship over at Lexington, otherwise, he'd be living at home and looking for a job. He's 21.

"My Dad's working full-time now at the turkey plant. Nights, so he can do some farm chores in the daytime. He's also sup-posedly doing something else that'll help---joined Gamblers Anonymous. Embarrassing, if you ask me. Mom drives him to meetings just to make sure he goes. She's taken away his phone, too."

Next week, Joey said, a "scavenger day" was planned at the farm. The bank contracted a company specializing in collect-ing smaller household goods---furniture, kitchen ware, cloth-ing, books, and lawn accessories. Then its people make a run through the property, carting away what might be worthwhile to several venues. These leftovers get sold at appropriate auc-tions or get carted away as trash.

"My parents are really squeezing us, my sister and brother. They're making us give up a lot of things. Every night when I go home they've found something to add to the pile. It's a 'new low' as far as I'm concerned."

And it was hard to argue. Then I did something that truly was a no-no if I'd given it thought at all. I got personally in-volved. It was a reflex action. I opened the gate with this: "If I can help in any feasible way, let me know."

The words barely left my mouth and Joey, sounding like this was the very reason for the visit, asked a favor. He wondered whether I could store a few of his prized possessions for him.

Huh?

He said, "My parents have gotten pretty paranoid about this. I guess I can't blame them. They're going through the house looking for anything that might be of value. Said we all have to contribute something. I've grabbed some souvenir stuff I really don't want to part with---sports jerseys, autographed baseballs, books, trophies, magazines, CDs, whatever. Stuff I've collected and really want to keep. I can't believe they'd be worth that much to anybody but me."

And?

"I've got everything in a couple of boxes. Right now, they're in the trunk of my car. My folks probably will stumble into them in the next few days. They're like a hurricane going through our rooms. Could you store them for me? Just for a few days. Then I'll take them off your hands. I promise."

Gulp.

Was I on shaky ground here? Was this any of my business? Could I get into trouble here?

"Not sure about this Joey. Can't you reason with your parents?"

Joey said, "Not really. I tried. They seem possessed. My sister already gave up some real treasures to her. She got into a big squabble with Mom and Dad. Tears and everything. They told her there was always a chance no one would be interested anyway. That didn't help. I don't want to take a chance. When I got home from work last night, I gathered up my things and packed them away. Hid them, really."

I had to get to a class and told Joey to return later. This gave me time for a call to Mary to explain the situation. I was prepared to take her advice.

I tracked her down in the student union grading papers over coffee. After explaining the situation, I popped the question. Should I get involved or not?

Her answer: "Hey, you're a department chair now. If you weren't, what would you do?"

"Probably help Joey out. He says he needs only a couple days, then he'll hide them somewhere else."

"Do it," she answered with this caveat. "You can always claim ignorance. Give him a strict time limit, though."

Two days, Joey agreed. I trusted him to keep that promise, but, as it turned out I would hang onto one item much longer.

Chapter 45

Discovery

Curiosity got the best of me, of course. After Joey delivered his two boxes to my office and they got tucked in my closet, I peeked. As expected, they were filled with personal items that could be of little value to anyone but Joey.

There was one exception. In a short stack of books at the bottom of a box, there was one with a title that sounded familiar---*"The Life of Washington"* by Mason L. Weems.

The leather covers were brownish with several tears, and leather-beaten finishes that were a tipoff this was a genuine oldie. The crinkly, stiff pages only served to further the impression. At the very least, it had to be a first edition.

The inside front cover read:

"A History of the Life and Death, Virtues, and Exploits of General George Washington with Curious Anecdotes Equally Honorable to Himself and Exemplary to His Young Countrymen."

Would it spoil the value that notes were scribbled throughout the pages? The handwriting was worn down to a faded, pencil-like penmanship that made words barely discernible. There were misspellings and, when words and partial sentences were legible, they did not always make sense. Grammar sucked, too.

In many ways, the book's beat-up, decrepit appearance seemed to enhance chances it could have unseen value. A first edition? Was that the thinking of Joey, too?

Americans were not especially literate in the early 1800s. Books were rare then and got passed around, a lot, which could account for the scribblings.

When he came to cart away his stash the next day, I asked Joey where he got it. "From the city library, at the end of the day when volunteers were told we could pick out a few books nobody wanted," he replied. "I showed it to Doctor Webber, but he kind of blew me off. Said it was junk. What do you think?"

My feelings? It was worth another inspection by an expert. I had just the person in mind: Carl Soggenheim, the Rotary speaker, Evansville antique store owner, and easily one of Indiana's leading Lincoln experts.

Even the state's historical society went to him for valuations. He was a walking eBay calculator. He had a specially fitted cell phone with software that would rate approximate values of objects.

"Sounds good to me," said Joey. "I kinda figured another opinion wouldn't hurt."

Chapter 46

Whoops

Carl Soggenheim had news for me. Good news.

"Thought I'd better call you first, give you the scoop," he said. "I'm not sure what it's going to finally mean, but the Lincoln book is apparently the real deal. Probably worth a lot. Everyone needs to move cautiously from this point. No announcements."

Carl had made the rounds with the Mason Weems' book all the way up from eBay to Sotheby's, and here was the shocker: Joey's copy of *"The Life of Washington"* was judged as a legitimate collectible. Experts and his other sources were unanimous this was the first book---at age eleven or twelve read by Abraham Lincoln.

"The tipoff was the handwritten scribbling," Carl relayed. "There are several distinctive parts to it---dotting the i's, crossing t's that sort of thing---that were perfect fits," he added. "And some of the phrases and descriptions that were underlined later became parts of his stump speeches and writing.

"There've been lots of forgeries through the years. If this is one, I've never seen a better one. Trust me."

For now, the *"Life of Washington"* by Mason Weems would remain locked up in the Indiana State Historical Society's vault in Indianapolis. Joey Burke, thrilled to get the news, was registered as the owner.

"How much is it worth?" was his first response when I broke the news to him. "This could not have happened at a better time. Man am I glad I grabbed that book."

Including Carl, we all agreed a plan needed to be put in place for Joey and his family. No doubt the book would be valuable. My minimal search described it as one of the real Lincoln gems yet to be found. And no doubt Joey was the owner, given that the book had been discarded and could be classified as ownerless trash.

It's value? We'd be talking six figures, according to Carl. "I'm just guessing, but I'd say you could get maybe $400,000, but be careful," he added. "There are a lot of sharks in this collectible business."

For now, Joey left finding a buyer in the hands of Carl and me. Carl was well known in the world of antiquities, and his reputation, from what I had learned, was impeccable. Quietly, he went shopping while we pledged to remain mum about the discovery. Only Jimmy, wrapping up a very successful basketball season at the University of Lexington, was left out of the circle.

"We don't want to do anything that'll throw him off his game," reasoned his dad, Pete.

"An artifact like this eventually needs to be open to the public, on display in a museum or library," said Carl. "Trouble is, not many institutions these days have the kind of money or endowments to match what it would bring on the open market. You hate to see these things fall into the hands of private collectors or investors, and nobody gets to see it."

Undoubtedly the Burkes had no interest in becoming collectors. Would it go to a private or public interest? They simply wanted the best price they could get.

If there was a loser in this saga, it had to be Professor Webber. You may recall that the prickly professor, drawing on his deep, self-appointed background as a PhD-bearing, tenured American history researcher and expert, had declared the book worthless. Thoroughly embarrassed at his misjudgment, he pulled me aside at one point with a favor to ask: Please leave his name out of any stories to be published in the *Hoosier-Record*, or anywhere else, about the book's discovery.

In a moment of weakness, I agreed. On the other hand, I expected his bumbling fumble to come in handy for leverage for my future academic committee proposals.

Chapter 47

Hoop Dreams

The Burke family was on a roll. Not long after the Lincoln book jackpot, the University of Lexington basketball team opened play in the NCAA men's tournament, arguably the most watched sports event in the U.S.---and traditionally a bettor's paradise.

The Thorobreds qualified for this first, historic (for them) appearance in the "Big Dance" by winning their conference playoffs. Unbelievably they took a seat alongside traditional powerhouses in the region such as Kentucky, Louisville, and Indiana. Jimmy Burke was a big reason for the success.

Despite its lowly 14th seeding, the Thorobreds opened with a stunning upset, sneaking by 2d seeded Texas A & M by an 83-81 score. Jimmy sealed that win on a three-point basket with two seconds remaining in the contest.

Lexington had been assigned to the regional tournament in Seattle. The victory advanced the Thorobreds into the round of 32 teams, pitting them against Tulane. Despite the distance from southern Indiana, the large, boisterous Lexington fans making the trip to the West Coast figured to be even louder in the second round.

It was all Pete Burke, and his family, could do to refrain from booking a flight and flying to Seattle, but no deals on the Lincoln book had yet to be finalized. Until then, their credit cards were no good.

They would've been disappointed by the results of the second-round game---a Lexington loss to Tulane, 91-82. Jimmy scored 20 points, one above his average, but uncharacteristically went 2-for-10 at the free throw line.

Amazingly, these tournament results appeared to make believers out of bettors. Or at least they did in Lexington's case, which saw the line (final margin) tightened by tipoff to the Thorobreds losing by only six points against number six Tulane. The day before the second round was to be played, Lexington was a 10-point underdog. A four-point jump in such a short time? Something was screwy.

Immediately, after that opening victory, rumors started spreading like dandelions in the spring. There was something funky about the outcome. How does a number 14 defeat a Number 2? This was one of several contests with startling upsets in the first round.

One answer to the Thorobred results might have been the man sitting in Seat 8, Section 14 of the Main Concourse of Seattle's Climate Pledge Arena. He kept to himself throughout the contests.

Maybe in his late 40s, he showed no allegiance to any of the schools in the competition. Instead, he kept copious notes throughout the action and engaged in lengthy cell phone calls at the conclusion of the games as the arena emptied.

An unemployed coach researching a job opening? A scout for one of the schools in the field? A scout for a professional team? Somehow, someway, he had to have a connection to the teams and players.

Chapter 48

The Fix Is On

Whistleblower: A person who informs on a person or organization engaged in an illicit activity.

While the Lincoln book adventure appeared headed for a happy ending, another story was brewing in the *Hoosier-Record* circulation area. This one did not appear headed for a happy ending.

A joint investigation by the FBI and IRS, concluding an entire winter of sleuthing, had uncovered evidence of illegal practices within its Princess Casino sports book. The Feds were following tips from at least one insider. No one outside the charges was quite sure of his or her identity, but it had to be someone familiar with Bel-Tar bookkeeping practices.

My guess was Pete Stanley, the Princess manager. Maybe he had help. In almost all of Pete's comments I heard, there seemed to be a tone of "moral disapproval" about his own industry. This was especially true if the subject was about better ways to capture a family audience.

Gambling, a family affair? Ugh.

The FBI left little doubt there was a tip from an inside source that led to this revelation: Business was very, very good in the

Bel-Tar fleet, but maybe too good. Some of those spectacular gains likely had nothing to do with luck. They came the old-fashioned way: Cheating. Or, in this case, fixing outcomes and individual performances.

"Pretty clever the way things worked," said Newt, who was given access to an FBI/IRS embargoed, preliminary briefing on the charges.

Using its power of subpoena, guided by additional whistle-blower tips---possibly by players, a close survey of individual Bel-Tar records brought this to light. The casino owners had a select number of college athletes---almost exclusively basket-ball, football players---on their employee payrolls.

And?

Well, for starters, just a few years earlier the link between active athletes and casino employment would have been a serious breach of NCAA rules, a real no-no. Student-athletes employed by a casino? While in season and actively playing? Unheard of. Now it was legal. Unbelievable.

Just think:

*That fumble at the goal line? Was the fumbler on the take to fix an outcome for his employer?

*The two missed free throws that would've sealed a victory? Was the athlete on the take to cut the scoring margin?

*The pass interference call when the defensive back barely touched the receiver? Was the referee on the take?

"The thing is," Newt said, "we're talking about kids 18 to the early 20s. They're the most vulnerable. They're around big money for the first time in their life. A few whispers from their casino employer, a little bonus on their paycheck, and that's all it takes. This is a great story. It could put my little news-paper on the map."

The new NCAA rules also allowed the jocks to have agents, which could only make things more volatile. "Think of it," said

Newt. "Just a few years ago the things athletes couldn't do now are perfectly legal. What's wrong with this picture?

"Oh, and let's not forget referees," he added. "They can be just as vulnerable. They can work in casinos, too. Or be in deep debt to them. Think they don't have personal problems that can get solved with a little payment under the table?"

Newt told me a great story that popped up in Kentucky when he worked in Louisville on the *Courier-Journal.* "There was this basketball game between two unrated colleges---I can't remember for sure who they were---and two of the three referees were on the take.

"And what made it hilarious? One official was trying to help one team and the other referee was helping the opposing team. When it was all done, the game set an NCAA record for total fouls."

College sports---and its shoddy record of enforcement--- was never known for scrupulous oversight. Their archaic compliance procedures relied on members to blow whistles on each other. Yeah. Sure.

According to U.S. FairPlay, a privately-owned, sports monitoring service that tracks irregularities for clients (a growth industry), there had been two dozen outcomes in the current school year that defied conventional odds. Bel-Tar "employees" who were on its payroll in uniform had erratic and/or inconsistent performances in 15 of those contests.

The list of anomalies also included two college football bowl games, at least one basketball contest in most power conferences and the same referee in three contests. Not one protest was voiced from a member school.

FairPlay people estimated that, on any given Saturday in football season, 8% of the games have a play that raises questions and warranted a closer look at the game. That would be at least five games per Saturday or approximately 15-18 per month. Because fewer players are needed, basketball is the most fertile competition for individual impact to alter a contest's statistics.

It pays to look closely. Most wagering is done through prop bets. Not wagering on simple winning and losing contests, but rather manipulating individual statistics and over-and-under team margins. Will Billy Butler hit his 16.6 points per game average? Will the scoring by Team A and Team B total more than 170 points?

Sometimes, the wagering gets absurd---how many timeouts will get called, total fumbles, total interceptions, official crowd size, which team controls the opening tip, total fouls, and penalties.

A Prairie Conference basketball game between Eastern Colorado and Southwest Kansas early last January? Who cared? This was a low-level Division 1 rivalry dominated by Eastern Colorado, which won the last six matchups in games never closer than 17 points.

The 294 fans in the EC field house in Lamar, Colorado, for the latest rematch could scarcely believe what transpired. Expected to make it another rout, their home team heroes barely survived 73-70 when its star player, Rocky Bridges, fouled out early in the second half with 11 points---10 below his average.

A pile of money exchanged hands on that otherwise obscure game, some of it headed Rocky's way. Oh, and Rocky works summers in a Las Vegas casino. There are bonuses to be earned when the athlete hits his mark and gets recorded as overtime pay on casino salary rolls. Sweet, eh?

There's no room for guilt. Once a player hits his (or her) mark and there's a payoff for, and from, the casinos, the athlete's hooked. Records are kept, including recordings of phone conversations with the unsuspecting athletes.

The government agents made the scenarios sound simple, yet it took a whistleblower within the system to sound the alert. The FBI, dipping into its ranks for sports-savvy agents, built some of its cases by scouting targeted games for inconsistencies during the regular season.

It was likely---but not publicized---the Bel-Tar involvement would result in a nice bundle for the whistleblower's effort. In addition to laws protecting whistleblowers, there are significant rewards commensurate with the stakes.

How much in this case? The government officials did not reveal a figure as it was too soon to learn. There had to be a conviction or settlement---but mid-six figures was a good estimate, a nice reward for reaching a moral high ground.

"If this person waited a while longer, it might've been a bigger payoff," reasoned Newt. "Maybe he or she had something immediate to solve. Needed to get out now."

Due to the busyness of the school year, plus the immense publicity the Princess Casino story would generate, I decided to keep my students away from this major story---for now. College trustees were sure to get a little nervous. There was no need to jeopardize our writing program. We would be treading in libelous territory.

Newt agreed. Of course, he carried *Hoosier-Record* articles plucked from wire services in addition to his own reporting and rewriting efforts. This was a huge story for local residents and circulation grew by several hundred new subscriptions.

The FBI/IRS would publicly announce the filing of charges with a full-blown press conference. This would be one week after the first round of the NCAA men's postseason playoffs. Basketball fever was in high gear and the story was sure to get great play in the media.

Chapter 49

Book Ends

Carl's search for a buyer of *"The Life of Washington"* by Mason L. Weems did not take as long as expected. Furthermore, his estimated price tag of "six figures" was right-on.

The book had two things going for it. In addition to its intrinsic value as the first book Lincoln read, which ranks right up there with possessing one of his stove pipe hats, there was this: It was a first edition that was over 200 years old. That does not happen often---no matter what the subject.

"That fact alone made it valuable, but nothing compared to being Old Abe's first," said Carl. "I say take the money and run. You don't want to find out later it's the second book he ever read."

How did it wind up among Harrison Public Library discards? Or, for that matter, how does a book in good shape last undiscovered and unprotected for 200 years?

"Beats me," said Carl. "That's something like six or seven generations it's passed through. That's got to be as old as anything coming out of this area unless you're talking dinosaurs. It's probably a good thing old Alva kept it locked up. That kept it safe."

No one knew Harrison library history better than Becky Barnes. She could shed no light on the mystery.

"I was there 25 of her 50 or so years, right next to Alva," said Becky. "She ran a very tight ship. She considered everything her personal property.

"It sounds silly to say, but in all that time I never once set foot in that back storage room. Well, once I tried ... the door was locked. I was new to the job. I asked Alva about access, what was in there. She chewed me out royally, pretty much letting me know I'd get fired if I set foot in there, and I needed this job.

"Who dropped it off? Your guesses are as good as mine. We can't be sure Alva knew.""

The Burkes, when informed of developments, could've cared less how the book made it to Joey. There were details and conditions to be resolved, but the buyer, thanks to Carl's deft negotiation, agreed to pay $325,000.

Milly burst into tears with the news. "Oh my god!" were her first words---between sobs. Pete, feeling faint, almost keeled over. "This means we can keep the farm," he said after catching his breath.

Yes, they could. The Harrison bank proved quick with paperwork that took the farm off the market. A new payment plan was structured. While it did not stretch far enough to give the family free and clear ownership, it did trim the overdue mortgage interest, and the bank created an affordable break on future payments. A chunk was set aside to take care of Joey's tuition.

Bank President Harold Jones became a local hero. He was happy to play the role of a good guy in this family drama but did whisper to a few associates the farm had created no interest in the real estate market.

And just who purchased the book?

He or she would remain anonymous. That's the way it often worked in the world of collectibles, according to Carl. This was especially true of private, individual buyers. They did not wish to be in the limelight. Apparently, it wasn't the Lincoln Presidential Library in Springfield, Illinois, which seemed to me a logical development.

On the other hand, it might be someone with Harrison College linkage. One condition of the deal was that it would be loaned to---and protected by---the college for public display for a "term to be decided." It would become the school's signature historical artifact---perfect for an unveiling when the new library is officially dedicated.

While I was not privy to the buyer's identity, I would've put my money on President Casey at least playing a role. The school was known to have several well-to-do alumni and a relatively fat---for a small liberal arts school---endowment.

I was sure the president would find a way to turn it into a profitable asset for the college.

Chapter 50

Stop the Presses

The FBI formally announced charges against Bel-Tar on Wednesday, which handed the TV networks a plum. This meant it was both a major, breaking news story as well as a timely topic for their Sunday morning talkfest panels.

Make no mistake. The NCAA's loosening of ties---and the hailstorm it created---was big news from coast to coast. Not only would it professionalize college sports for athletes, but it also had the potential to create wide-open doors for the gambling industry. Television stations, both local and network, flocked to the press conference scheduled for the Harrison County Courthouse.

Why in Harrison and not a federal building in Indianapolis or Louisville? Or Lexington, for that matter? Though it never would be admitted, the Feds liked the idea of making things easy for TV and other graphic-oriented media. The courthouse location meant out-of-town press could easily swing by and add pictures of the anchored Princess Casino only a few miles away on the Ohio River.

Since the Princess was a major player in the charges, what better way to help tarnish its image than to make sure the public had a visual of the bad guy? And hey, If Bel-Tar was fixing sports outcomes, who's to say that its roulette wheels, slot machines, and card games were on the square?

Of course, Newt was especially happy the press conference would take place in the Harrison courthouse. This was just across the street from his *Hoosier-Record* office on the square. Nothing like starting a week with a big news story dropped in your lap.

But he wasn't quite prepared for what greeted him on that memorable Wednesday. For starters, the only parking he could find was three blocks away from his usual spot in front of the *Hoosier-Record* office. The square was jammed.

Almost every daily newspaper within 150 miles, including Louisville, Bloomington, and Indianapolis, had reporters and photographers covering the announcement. Four large TV trucks with satellite dishes on the roof took up a good share of the space. At least five TV cameras and crew would be positioned in a cluster around the podium.

Local business owners, especially those on the square, were shocked to turn a corner and find themselves in a traffic jam with these out-of-town vehicles---and few parking spots available as early as 7 a.m.

The FBI's pre-press conference hint of a big story involving the Princess Casino, gambling improprieties, and pro and college sports outcomes proved irresistible to newshounds. Something like this had been rumored, expected really, ever since the NCAA loosened the rules of eligibility over a year ago.

After uncharacteristically standing in line for five minutes, Newt and I, finally got a booth at the *Dough Girls* coffee bar a half-hour before the courthouse doors opened. Never before were we unable to get immediate seating. The din was deafening. We were practically shouting at each other after we took seats.

"What gives?" asked co-owner Marge, pressed into duty as a waitress from her usual spot at the cash register. "We've never had this kind of crush. This is bigger than the President's Day parade crowd.

"Mostly strangers, too. Hope this doesn't scare away regulars. We might run out of doughnuts and coffee. Good thing it's Wednesday instead of Friday. That's when we start running out of everything."

We assured Marge this was likely to be a one-day splash. Though we didn't know details about the announcement, the FBI did leak that charges were related to sports and gambling. Who would've thought the first shoe would fall in an out-of-the-way Harrison? For sure the local college, which played in lower NCAA Division Three, was not a major player in this national drama.

"You mean all these customers are news people?" she asked. "Thought I recognized one guy, a TV reporter from Evansville. He looked a little different without makeup. I better start smiling. Might get some free publicity."

In the end, this news media entourage got what it came for in Harrison. Fixed sporting events? NCAA rules being violated? You bet, according to the FBI. A long list of alleged infractions was made public. They couldn't miss, though there were some tricky legalities to be explained to viewers and readers. These would be Federal charges, too. State borders were crossed.

The first wave of press conference reportage came from TV stations and web sites an hour after the Q & A. There was liberal use of graphics shot at the casino entrance. Cameras were not allowed inside the boat.

Reporters were doing man-on-the-street interviews with anyone they saw in Harrison and at the casino entrance---but ended up trashing most of this footage. What a laugh. The interviewees had no idea what the interviewers were talking about.

The print media---from the New York Times to the Kokomo Tribune--- displayed the story with more depth. A handful of reporters from this wave, unencumbered by cameras and cameramen, also parked themselves at the casino entrance and were luckier.

In one case, a supposed casino employee on his way to work, made memorable comments after granted anonymity. Later, it was revealed the interview was bogus. The interviewee, after asking the interviewer for an autograph, was unmasked as a customer headed for the slots.

One enterprising *Indianapolis Star* reporter fanned out and made it to the Harrison College campus for input. Turned out she also was looking to hook up with her son, a junior, for possible guidance into the faculty ranks for some story context. A faculty expert on gambling? Why not? There were plenty of faculty willing to fake it just to get some airtime. Got to have it. Instead, she was directed to me.

"My son says your classes write stories that get published in the local newspaper," she said after I opened my office door to her knock. "I'd love to pick your brain on some meaningful people to interview; people that live here."

I was tempted to refer her to Professor Webber, who had been spotted several times in the Princess at the card tables. I didn't. I figured he'd been embarrassed enough with his monumental goof of dismissing the Lincoln book.

I was careful not to reveal inside details, but I'm not sure the reporter really cared. Generic quotes. That was OK with her. She simply needed any comments to justify expenses and a visit with her son.

It took the *Hoosier-Record* to set things straight. Granted, it was a little easier for a weekly newspaper. There are no hourly and daily deadlines causing panic and reporting sketchy information. A weekly had several days to talk to people and collect content to add more insight to the story.

Newt put several of my students to work gathering material for his Friday publication, when he would jump into the story with---hopefully---a truly in-depth article covering up-to-date developments. There would be several sidebars, presumably something by Craig Marshall, who'd been snooping around the casino the entire school year.

"I got a feeling this story's going to have a lot of readers for me, and not just locals," said Newt, who hiked his press run an extra 250 copies. "We're sort of the launching pad for one of the largest scandals in college sports and this is college sports country."

Newt didn't say it, but his reputation among peers on large newspapers definitely added credibility to anything his *Hoosier-Record* would publish. In addition to being a prize-winning journalist in Louisville and cracking big stories, his efforts in resurrecting struggling local journalism had a growing audience among the smarter editors.

Surely his lead story would be read closely.

The scandal grew and grew. Nervous athletic directors and coaches, now worried their athletes were involved in fixing outcomes, scrambled madly to film rooms to inspect games and individual performances. Any jocks on casino employment rolls became prime suspects. Names started getting mentioned. So were schools such as Memphis, Nevada-Las Vegas, Kentucky, and Arizona.

Business boomed for U.S. FairPlay, the consulting firm that studies sports anomalies. It hired a half-dozen new investigators---several former CIA agents---to handle the crush. In the case of college basketball, only a few NCAA playoff games remained in the season but no problem. No sport---golf, baseball, tennis, hockey, soccer, etc.---would escape scrutiny.

The FBI inspected rules being broken that had inter-state ties. State officials jumped on intra-state cases whereby suspected crimes were committed in the same state as the casino paying the athlete. Bel-Tar was hit especially hard, easily outdistancing other casinos on the college basketball and football side.

Nearly a dozen student-athletes were, or had been, employed by its four casinos as part-time "greeters." Not coincidentally, salary bonuses---$1,000 and up---frequently got noted on their pay checks. A simple check of dates when the bonuses were earned always coincided with a game in their sport.

The Internal Revenue Service (IRS) piled on, eventually opening a specific, separate case against Bel-Tar. The great surge in the Princess revenues created such an unexpected, giant tax bill in its Indiana port that chunks of cash were funneled to its three Kentucky-anchored casino boats, where gambling on sports events was not yet legal and taxes were low. Government accountants estimated the laundering scheme was worth $1 million to the Detroit-based syndicate.

Chapter 51

Jimmy's Future

Our little Harrison College was a spectator in the on-going, ever-expanding national, drama, watching major college athletic departments, sports agents, and student-athletes self-destruct. Lawsuits were falling like raindrops. Who knew there were that many lawyers?

Whitey loved it. On my few visits to his tavern, I noticed a slight uptick in his business. "Yeah, got to be some fallout from the Princess in all this," he said. "This keeps up, and I'm going to start selling lottery tickets."

Some Harrison faculty in sociology and American Studies were making plans to incorporate elements into their classes in the next school year. For sure, I would have my writing class do stories then, too. The story broke too late to tackle in the current academic year, though several returnees were bugging me to do an Independent Study on it over the summer.

Perhaps the one person I expected not to be upbeat was Joey Burke. The transaction on the Lincoln-read book, *The Life of Washington*, was nearly completed. The Harrison bank and his parents had finalized an agreement. The family could go to bed at night without fearing what the next day would bring and, important to him, future tuition problems would not be a problem. He could quit working at the turkey processing plant.

Furthermore, as far as anyone knew, his father, Pete, had perfect attendance at his GA meetings. "How could I gamble when I might be betting against my own kid?" he would say to Milly.

One piece in the puzzle remained for Joey, however. I was destined to learn more when he knocked on my office door late one afternoon.

"I got to tell someone, but not my folks," he said, after we exchanged a few pleasantries. "They've suffered through enough already."

What's the problem?

"It's Jimmy. I'm nervous for him. Have you noticed his name hasn't popped up in the scandal? He works at one of the Bel-Tar boats over in Kentucky and he's a big part of the Lexington team, yet he missed a lot of free throws in the tournament at Seattle.

"He's coming home tomorrow morning for the first time in several months, and I'm worried. He called last night and wants to meet me before he sees Mom and Dad. Says he's got something important to tell me. I'm scared shitless he's mixed up in this Bel-Tar business. That'll kill our folks. We finally dug ourselves out of a hole, now may have another problem."

The rendezvous? The *Dough Girls Bakery and Café*, naturally. Jimmy was already in a booth and wolfing down a second order of pancakes when Joey arrived.

"Damn, I miss this place," was Jimmy's immediate greeting as he stood to hug his brother. "Nothing like it in Lexington, bro. I'd be 15 pounds overweight if there was."

The brothers sat, exchanged pleasantries for a few minutes. Jimmy was especially interested in updates on Harrison High School classmates. Only three years separated them in school.

In a town as small as Harrison, there were few secrets among any and all alums.

Then the subject turned to Jimmy's experiences at the University of Lexington.

"Everybody in town followed your every basketball move," said Joey. "It was really something. No one could remember anybody from Harrison playing---starting, too---in the NCAA tournament. Too bad it came to an end, but you guys won one game and that was something. A big upset, too."

Replied Jimmy, "Yeah, I think we could've beat Tulane at least five times if we played 10 games. I couldn't believe I missed so many free throws. Don't know if that made a difference or not."

The pause was palpable.

"Yeah, I know what people are saying," said Jimmy, breaking the silence. "I'm reading the newspapers and watching TV just like everyone else. All I can say is our team was legit. I know it doesn't look good, but we were legit. I worked for Bel-Tar last summer, but I never got asked to do anything crooked. I won't either. I'm quitting that job."

Joey's reaction? He looked like a 100-pound sack of turkey feathers had been lifted off his shoulders. "That's a good idea," he responded. "I think you want to be as far from casinos as you can get considering what it's done to our family."

Jimmy wasn't finished. "Glad you said that. I also want to transfer out of Lexington, too. That's what I want to break the news on. Maybe take a year off, get a job, and help with family finances. I'm tired of watching everyone else make sacrifices while I'm still playing sports. My scholarship doesn't cover everything.

"After taking a year off, I don't think I'd have a problem finding a new school to get a scholarship. Heck. Maybe I'd enroll at Harrison College and live at home like you. I could always play basketball here. No athletic scholarships at Division 3 schools, but what do I care? I'll never play in the NBA."

Joey didn't know where to start. The $300,000-plus pay-off to the Burkes and the story behind it had been kept from Jimmy up to this point. There had been no public announcement or news story on the book's discovery. Acting on Carl Soggenheim's advice, only a tight knot of insiders knew. It would stay that way until all details surrounding the transaction were finalized---probably in a few weeks.

"We didn't want anything to distract you during the season," explained Joey. "We planned a little homecoming party for you tonight. I don't know if this changes your future plans, but I'd say we're headed for a happy ending one way or another."

Happy homecoming? That would be putting it mildly. It was one for the books.

Chapter 52

Commencement

It was a bright, sunny Saturday. The prayers of the Harrison College maintenance department were answered.

The formal Commencement Day ceremony is always scheduled to be held outdoors on the Young Stadium football field, but rain, or even the threat, could cause a last-minute scramble of plans. That meant moving the chairs, decorations, sound system and portable stage into the adjacent fieldhouse.

"The sun always shines on our campus," President Casey liked to tell everyone on this special day. And, in fact, the weather had been drop-dead gorgeous for all five of the ceremonies in his tenure. I checked.

This was a time for the faculty PhDs to show their three stripes and alma mater colors on their robes. No one seemingly got into the spirit quite like Dr. Webber. He flapped his three-striped sleeves like a bird trying for liftoff every time he walked across the stage.

For me, it's a hoot to don a cap and gown. Not that long ago, I was on the receiving end of my first college diploma---a Bachelor of Arts (BA) in English. Now I was up to two stripes on my sleeve as possessor of a Master of Fine Arts (MFA) degree in creative writing---a terminal rank for me in the world of higher education.

No way was I going to return to school as a student to get a PhD. Hey, I'm a department chair. On the other hand, who knows?

Dr. Brand, the master of ceremonies, was a wise speaker. He knew to keep his remarks short. By now, many parents had grown weary of the campus, and their four years of tuition payments and trips to Harrison for special events. They were anxious to get a head start for home and get their kid into the next phase of life---hopefully the workforce with a competitive salary.

In past years, keynote speakers did not always keep it short, especially those who saw an opportunity to plug a book or some special interest. This year's speaker definitely kept it short.

In his continued effort to woo Chinese resources and students, President Casey arranged for a principal speaker named Chan Tai Man to receive an honorary degree. Officially he was only a second-tier bureaucrat in China's U.S. Embassy, but he was known as someone quite partial to building strong links between his homeland and the U.S. His specialty was student and faculty exchanges.

Chan had no real connection with Harrison. He'd never been on the campus before this event. Undoubtedly, he'd never been in Indiana. His English was almost non-existent. He drew a laugh when, in one fumbled attempt to speak our language, he referred to President Casey as having been "a skilled liar" instead of "a skilled lawyer" before Jonathan took the Harrison reins. The translator at Chan's side quickly made a correction, and his remaining comments were short, sweet, and totally appropriate.

If there was a downer on the stage, it was seeing Dr. Schackelford---my predecessor as head of the English Department. He looked terrible. Ashen, weak, wasted, limping and using a cane as he made it to the stage to receive his Professor Emeritus Award. He got a standing ovation.

I felt guilty seeing him in such sad shape. It had been several months since we had visited in his home. I still had not paid that visit two weeks later, when word reached me of the good professor's passing. Shame on me.

There were many positive things for the president to note about the school year, more than I could recall cited at my previous Harrison commencements. There was no mention of the festering casino issue, which was headed for a long resolution in the courts and really did not have a connection with our college.

The big ticket appeared to be a formal announcement of a new college capital drive. This one was to fund a major overhaul of the athletic facilities now that the science and technology project was near completion. It would include the addition of an indoor swimming pool, something many students and alumni considered a gaping hole that needed filling.

In recounting the school year, the president included glowing remarks about the successful library merger. This was news to some in the audience, of course. He called it a wonderful example of collaboration between the college and community.

Wisely, he had one more surprise saved for his conclusion. Reaching underneath the podium and pulling out a box, he reached into it and held up the contents: a book, "*The Life of Washington*" by Mason L. Weems.

While some in the crowd had followed the adventures surrounding its acquisition as reported in the *Hoosier-Record* and other media, no one was aware up to this point that it would be landing, and on display, in the school's newly merged library. This was not public knowledge.

Not only would it be on display for public viewing, Harrison College was formulating plans for it to become a major attraction for history buffs. This effort would be boosted by its official "landmark status" certification with official provenance provided by the U.S. National Park Service.

There will be no charge for public viewing, President Casey explained, but *The Life of Washington* by Pastor Weems would become a catalyst for several campus initiatives.

For starters, it will become a centerpiece in library space that would become a mini museum concentrating on southern Indiana history. Next, credit courses in my English and the history departments would be devoted to the book as well as a noncredit class in the school's adult online offerings.

Last, but not least, President Casey added that it will be the centerpiece for a yearly "Lincoln Conference" on the campus for history buffs. This would be sponsored by the Indiana Historical Society and figured to create a revenue stream.

There are hundreds of yearly Lincoln events in the U.S., topped by Illinois' bulging calendar and the location of the ex-president's official library. But the college's possession of the Weems book, plus its locale in the heart of where he spent formative years, would add much as an attraction.

"Just standing here and holding a book read by Abraham Lincoln gives me shivers," the president concluded. This remark drew snickers. It was 89 degrees and muggy when he said it.

"The historical significance and attraction of this book---the first one ever read by President Abraham Lincoln---is obvious, of course," the president said in his commencement remarks. "What won't be as obvious to the public is this: the great collaborative effort behind its acquisition by Harrison College."

While some in the audience were aware of the book saga, President Casey's update filled in unknown details. I knew that when I saw Newt, sitting several rows from the front, take a notebook to scribble some notes.

Chapter 53

Sweet Sorrow

With the school year's conclusion at hand and summer break on the immediate horizon, one mystery lingered for me. How would Mary and I proceed---gulp---as a couple? Considering that for the past three years, her apartment was above mine in the same off-campus building, clearly, some adjustments were now in order.

No question that with Mary headed for Tempe and her new position, Harrison would become history. It wouldn't take long for her to get settled into Arizona State University digs. She had several friends from her student days there ready to put her up while she located an apartment.

"Don't sweat it, big boy," she assured. "I'll make sure, ahcm, it'll be large enough to accommodate a guest."

Her ASU courses did not begin for several months, but Mary wanted to get started soon prepping for classwork. Knowing her, even the prep would be an all-out effort. She already had a handle on her schedule, classroom, and a list of early signees for her courses.

One graduate degree-level class would be an overview of Immigration Studies. This would entail assisting grad students on credit-earning, PhD-related research projects. The other course would be an undergrad, introductory sociology class that was part of a new interdisciplinary program.

"The undergrad bit actually gets me most excited," she said. "I'm told early registration shows this will be something new for my kids. I like that. No pre-conceived biases. Maybe I can knock down some doors for them. The dean says he wants me to give them a heavy dose of migratory and border issues, not just with Mexico, but globally."

In the past, when my summers were clear, I tagged along with Mary to Tempe and did volunteer work for a couple months--- teaching, working soup kitchens, urban gardening, those sorts of things---for a Catholic settlement house. She did research. Now as a department chair, and even though it was on an interim basis, I'd be anchored in Harrison much of the summer with lots of new administrative duties. Bureaucracy at work.

The passing year had not exactly been chopped liver, of course. I had started looking forward to just teaching classes, introducing a new writing course, organizing some independent study projects, and strengthening a connection with outside news outlets for writing ---namely the *Hoosier*-Record for grooming some of my brighter students.

No way could I have figured on becoming a department chair, play an important role in Abraham Lincoln's life, and getting caught up in a major story like the fixing of college and professional basketball and football games.

"So, where do we go from here, considering you'll be in southern Indiana and I'm in Tempe?" Mary asked.

"Well, there'll be some long weekends. One of us can jump on an airplane. I will be taking most of July off and I assume you can get away for a few weeks occasionally," was my answer. "Fact is, we don't see each other all that much when we're together in either place."

Of course, there would be this: would being married, something we both knew at this point was a distinct possibility, be a solution?

Not really. The logistics would remain the same as this summer. We'd reunite when there were holidays and one of us squeezed out an occasional 3-day weekend. The Indianapolis airport was only a couple hours from Harrison while the ASU campus was practically on the Phoenix airport runway.

If I got the department chair position on a permanent basis after this year, things would not change at my end for another five years. We'd have to deal with that bridge when we came to it. Meanwhile, our American Airlines Mileage-Plus accounts were the big winner.

A week following the Harrison College commencement our hugs and kisses at the Indianapolis Airport were a little tighter, more heartfelt. The immediate plan was for me to drive Mary to her flight, then she would carry as much luggage---mostly clothing---as she could jam into two suitcases.

Several weeks later, I would jam in her car what remained in her Harrison apartment, mostly files. Then I'd drive to Tempe, where, hopefully, she would have housing finalized. This was not exactly a farewell for us, but no question somewhere out there, a clock was ticking a little quicker.

About the Author

Mike Conklin is a storyteller. He's written professionally for audiences since high school, where his media career started with a small-town weekly. He graduated to local and regional dailies, and, following a cup of coffee in TV & Radio broadcasting, made a long stop at The Chicago Tribune. There, he was a beat reporter, daily columnist, and feature writer with work nationally syndicated. Mike's also written for the New York Times, a variety of magazines, reviewed books, and, after leaving The Tribune, taught full-time at Chicago's DePaul University, where he took leaves to teach at other universities and colleges in the U.S. and China. Now, drawing on a kitbag full of experiences and characters, an eye for an entertaining narrative, and equal parts imagination, he writes novels. *"He Bet The Farm"* is his fourth. Others were: *"Goal Fever!"*, *"Transfer U."* and *"Class Dismissed."*

Acknowledgements

Many sources have been helpful in writing *"He Bet The Farm"* and none was more important to me than Diane, my wife. A member of three book clubs, her feel for good writing, editing, and workable narratives is---and has been---invaluable. Also, another big thanks to James Elsener, a former Chicago Tribune colleague. A good novelist himself, his suggestions have plugged a lot of holes in my writing.

Printed in the USA
CPSIA information can be obtained
at www.ICGtesting.com
LVHW010729080324
773805LV00039B/260

9 781958 943991